The Secret of Witch Cottage

Amanda Wills

ISBN: 1540612716
ISBN-13: 978-1540612717

CHAPTER 1

Poppy McKeever squinted into the sun, her eyes
never leaving her best friend Scarlett as she cantered
off towards the horizon. Scarlett's shoulders were stiff
and unyielding, in contrast to her loose ponytail of
auburn curls, which bounced jauntily on her back
with every stride. Her Dartmoor pony Blaze was
growing smaller by the minute. Which was ironic,
Poppy thought wryly, as that had been the catalyst for
their row. Cloud stamped an impatient foot, desperate
to gallop after them, but she ran a hand down his
neck and shook her head.

"Let them go. She'll come round once she's had a
chance to cool off. Drama queen," she added under
her breath.

Cloud gave a tremulous whinny.

"She'll be fine. All I did was tell her that she looked
like a drum on a pea when she rode Blaze these days.
It was meant to be a joke and she totally over-reacted.
Ridiculous."

Poppy sighed. On reflection, it had sounded pretty

mean. And she felt a small sliver of remorse as she remembered Scarlett's last words before she'd taken flight.

"I know I'm too big for Blaze, Poppy. You don't have to rub it in. It's alright for you. You've got Cloud. Mum and Dad have already told me they can't afford another pony. It's Blaze or nothing."

Poppy had tried to backtrack but Scarlett, her eyes shining with unshed tears, had held her hand up to silence her.

"Save your breath. I'm not interested. I'm going home." And she had wheeled Blaze around and kicked her into a canter, leaving Poppy gaping at her retreating back, completely lost for words. It was only when Blaze had disappeared that Poppy realised she didn't know the way home. Bored with their usual rides, Scarlett had taken them on a new route across the high, open moorland towards Princetown. Poppy loved the bleak, windswept panoramas they had crossed, but landmarks were few and far between and one craggy tor looked much like another. She patted the pocket in which she kept her mobile but pride stopped her from phoning Scarlett.

"We can find our way home, can't we Cloud?" The Connemara flicked an ear back and stamped his foot again. Poppy gathered his reins and clicked her tongue. "Come on, let's go."

Before long the wide, stony path split in two. The first track was deeply rutted and lined with a gorse hedge and veered off sharply to the left. The second path was narrower and less well trodden and led in arrow-like precision towards a cluster of conifers straight ahead.

Poppy glanced over her shoulder. She could just make out the high granite walls of HMP Dartmoor. The impenetrable building, constructed two centuries before to hold prisoners of the Napoleonic Wars, dominated the skyline on this part of the moor. Her brother Charlie was fixated with the prison and had a ghoulish fascination for stories about the many convicts who'd escaped over the years.

"If Princetown is behind us, we must be facing east, so I think we need to follow the farm track," Poppy said. Cloud was sniffing the wind, his nostrils flared and his eyes fixed on the conifers. He whinnied again, the tremors shuddering along his dappled grey body like a mini earthquake. Perhaps he'd caught the faintest scent of Blaze and the chestnut mare was ahead, hidden from sight in the trees. Poppy trusted her pony implicitly. After all, he had roamed wild on the moor for years. If he couldn't lead her home to Riverdale, no-one could.

She gave him his head and he stepped onto the narrow path. It was a gloriously sunny afternoon in the middle of August yet the ground was still boggy in places. Poppy admired the way Cloud instinctively avoided the squelching peat by sticking to the grassy tussocks. At the edge of the band of trees the grass gave way to a carpet of rust-coloured pine needles and pine cones and when the path petered out Cloud kept walking, his ears pricked and his eyes still fixed ahead.

The deeper they walked into the trees the more the light leached away like sand in an hourglass. It was as if someone had pressed fast-forward to dusk. Charlie would say the shadowy forest was a perfect place for escaped prisoners to hide. Poppy shivered in her thin cotton tee-shirt.

They skirted a fallen tree and a clump of acid-green forest ferns. Poppy twiddled with a length of Cloud's silver mane.

"Are you *sure* this is the right way?" she said. But Cloud ploughed on through the towering conifers. Scratchy branches grazed Poppy's bare arms and the scent of pine needles filled her nostrils.

"Scarlett!" she yelled. "Are you there?" Poppy cocked her head to listen for an answering shout, but the only sound was the static-like crackle of Cloud's hooves hitting the forest floor. "Ridiculous!" she muttered again, as a branch caught her cheek. She was sure Scarlett would never have ridden this way home. But they had come so far she was curious to see what lay beyond the trees, and why Cloud was so intent on leading her there.

Gradually the gaps between the conifers widened and the sunlight streamed through the green canopy once again. Cloud stepped out onto open moorland, sniffed the wind and whickered softly. Poppy gazed around in astonishment.

"This is *beautiful*," she breathed.

The small forest of evergreens concealed a teardrop-shaped tarn, on the banks of which stood a tumbledown cottage. A dry stone wall circled the cottage like a granite necklace. Poppy slithered to the ground and laced her fingers in Cloud's mane. He whickered again and began walking resolutely ahead.

"Wait! We don't know who lives here," she whispered, tugging his reins. She stared at the cottage, looking for signs of life, aware they could be trespassing on private property. What if it was the home of a terse old hill farmer, with a distrust of strangers and a shotgun under the bed? Poppy's eyes travelled over the building, taking in the gaping hole in the catslide roof, the front door hanging off its ancient hinges and the rotting wooden window frames. She realised that the cottage must have been abandoned decades ago. Cloud strained forwards and Poppy finally relented.

"You win," she told him. "We'll go and explore."

The cottage was tiny, as small as a shepherd's croft. A battalion of nettles, heavy with tiny white flowers, guarded the front door. Poppy looped Cloud's reins over an old fence post, edged past the nettles and gave the door a tentative push. It swung inwards, hitting the wall with a clatter. She took a deep breath and stepped over the threshold.

The front door led straight into a small, empty square room that Poppy supposed must once have been the parlour. The air smelt fusty, as if it hadn't been disturbed in years, and when she ran her fingers along the windowsill they picked up a layer of fine, sooty dust. Blackened beams intersected the low ceiling and the uneven floor was laid with cracked and stained quarry tiles in shades of sienna and ochre. On the outside wall was a fireplace with a granite hearth and a simple wooden mantelpiece. Opposite the fireplace was another door. Poppy tugged at the tarnished brass handle.

The kitchen was even smaller than the parlour and was also empty apart from a stone sink under the window and a rusty range. A creaky narrow staircase led to two tiny rooms in the eaves. Poppy inched her way across the woodworm-ridden floorboards in the larger of the two bedrooms to the window to check

Cloud was still happy nibbling grass where she'd left him. A movement in the corner of her eye made her jump, but it was only a swallow, swooping out of a gap in the roof towards the still waters of the tarn. Hearing high-pitched cheeping, Poppy craned her neck and saw four baby swallows peeking out of their mud nest tucked under the eaves.

An old hessian sack had been tossed into one corner and two wooden crates were arranged in the middle of the floor facing the window. Almost like chairs, it occurred to Poppy. The silence in the old cottage was absolute. She wondered what kind of person would choose to live such a remote and lonely life so high on the moor. She gazed at the sloping ceilings and uneven walls, but the cottage wasn't giving away any of its secrets.

Feeling a sneeze looming, Poppy tramped back down the stairs. Cloud lifted his head as she emerged into the sunlight and she unhooked his reins and led him to the water's edge. He grazed while she threw stones into the dark water of the tarn, enjoying the ripples they made as they sank out of sight. Cloud seemed so at ease Poppy was sure it wasn't the first time he had been to the cottage.

"This place is so cool. Charlie and Scarlett will love it," she said, before remembering that Scarlett wasn't talking to her. Poppy's earlier irritation had waned, to be replaced by an anxious knot in her stomach. She hated conflict and usually avoided it at all costs. She knew Scarlett was devastated that she had almost outgrown her beloved Blaze and was gutted that her parents couldn't afford another pony. It was hardly surprising she'd had a serious sense of humour failure. Poppy wished she could turn back the clock. Falling out with her best friend in the middle of the summer holidays was the last thing she wanted to do. She reached for her mobile and tapped out a quick text.

Sorry Scar, didn't mean to upset you. Still BFF???

But the screen remained stubbornly blank. After half an hour of checking and re-checking her phone she admitted defeat, dragged herself to her feet and swung back into the saddle. She and Cloud re-traced their steps back through the conifers.

"This time we'll go my way," she said, turning him down the gorse-lined farm track to their right. "These tractor tracks must lead somewhere."

The track climbed steadily until Poppy could see over the band of conifers to the cottage and lake below. After a couple of miles the track became even more rutted. The gorse bushes were replaced by an old stone wall, which they followed for another mile or so to a farm tucked in the hollow between two tors. The farmyard was deserted, save for a couple of bantams scratching around in the dirt. When the track merged with a tarmac lane Poppy squeezed Cloud into a trot. Eventually they reached a staggered crossroads and a lichen-covered sign. *Waterby four miles.*

Poppy wondered if Scarlett was still seething at her thoughtless jibe. She could kick herself for being so insensitive. As she turned Cloud towards home one thing dominated her thoughts. How could she make amends?

CHAPTER 2

The next morning Poppy found Charlie helping Caroline stick labels onto dozens of jars of homemade raspberry and strawberry jam.

"You haven't forgotten it's the fete today?" Caroline mumbled, a pen between her teeth.

Poppy groaned. "Do I have to come?"

"You promised to do pony rides, remember? Cloud's one of the star attractions. You can't let all those children down," her stepmother said.

Poppy pulled a face. "He's not a novice ride. Some awful screaming toddler is bound to fall off and end up with concussion. And then I'll be sued. I don't think I should go."

"No-one is going to fall off. Cloud will be on the leadrope and the children will be wearing hats. You never know, you might even enjoy it," Caroline said.

Charlie licked a label and smoothed it onto a jar of strawberry jam.

"Charlie, that's disgusting!" Poppy shrieked.

"Someone got out of bed the wrong side this

morning," said Charlie, smoothing out the air bubbles with his thumbs.

Poppy shot him a filthy look and slammed two pieces of bread in the toaster. She had woken up grumpy and her mood hadn't improved when there was still no text or missed call from Scarlett. At least her best friend had agreed to help with the pony rides, giving Poppy a chance to apologise face to face.

The phone rang. Caroline stuck the pen behind her ear and answered it.

"Hello Pat! Yes, the tombola's done and we've almost finished the jam. We just need to load the car and we're ready. Poppy will ride Cloud over and meet us there." There was a pause. Caroline frowned. "Oh, that's a shame. I hope she feels better soon. Give her our love, won't you?"

"What's happened?" Poppy demanded.

"Scarlett's not feeling too well. She's decided not to come."

Poppy gouged a piece of butter from the tub and began attacking her toast. "Just brilliant," she grumbled.

"Why *are* you in such a bad mood?" said Charlie, who had finished packing the jam into cardboard boxes and was counting the float.

"I. Am. Not. In. A. Bad. Mood," Poppy growled. But Charlie wasn't listening. His eyes had taken on a faraway look and a smile was tugging at the corners of his mouth.

"Mum, do we have any brown wool?"

"I expect so. Have a look in the dresser."

Charlie scrabbled around in a drawer and pulled out a ball of soft, mocha-brown wool.

"Perfect," he said.

Despite herself, Poppy was curious. "What do you want it for?"

"You know I'm doing pin a tail on the donkey for the Canvas Challenge?"

Poppy nodded. Charlie's Cub pack had launched an appeal to raise money to buy new camping equipment to replace its leaky tents. Charlie had spent the last week tracing out and colouring in a huge, lop-sided donkey which he'd pinned to a cork board and planned to set up on an old easel Caroline had found in the loft. Blindfolded fete-goers would be invited to try their hand at pinning the tail on the donkey for fifty pence a go, and anyone who managed to pin the tail anywhere near its backside would win a plastic cup of sweets.

"I'm going to do a 3D version," he announced.

Now Charlie was a dab hand with Lego but Poppy sincerely doubted that even he could knock up a donkey in the hour they had before they had to set off for the fete.

"I just need to make a tail out of this," he said, waving the wool in Poppy's face, "and check Chester's nice and clean and we're in business."

Poppy almost choked on a mouthful of toast.

"You are *not* using Chester for pin the tail on the donkey!" she screeched. "Are you *mad*?"

"Why not? Chester loves children and he's too old for donkey rides."

"You can't have people sticking drawing pins into him. It's animal cruelty!"

Charlie gave her a withering look. "I wouldn't use drawing pins, grumpy-pants. I'm not that stupid. We've got some double-sided sticky tape in the craft box. I'll use that instead."

Caroline held up her hands. "That's enough, you two. How about a compromise? We bring Chester along to the fete so children can make a fuss of him, but we use Charlie's lovely picture to pin the tail on. I can still make you a wool tail if you want, Charlie?"

Appeased, Charlie nodded.

"We'll leave at nine. That'll give us plenty of time to set the stall up before the fete opens at ten," said Caroline.

The annual Waterby summer fete, held on the third Saturday in August, was one of the highlights of the village's social calendar, eclipsed only by the Christmas Eve nativity service, which drew people from far and wide. The nativity boasted real animals in a lovingly re-created Bethlehem stable at the front of the church. More impressive still, the youngest babe-in-arms in the parish was always given the honour of playing Jesus. One especially memorable year, when there had been a shortage of babies, the job had been given to a wilful eighteen-month-old toddler called Isaac, who had thrown his swaddling cloth off just as the Three Kings arrived, climbed out of the manger, pointed at Mary and bawled, "That's not my mummy!" It had made headlines in the Tavistock Herald.

Every group in the village ran a stall at the summer fete to raise funds for their own organisation and the competition to outdo each other was fierce. Caroline had been roped into running the tombola for Charlie's school's PTA, and had, through a combination of cajoling and coercion, amassed a vast array of prizes, from cans of fizzy drink and bottles of bubble bath to food hampers and, the star prize, a digital camera.

When Caroline had first asked Poppy if she and Scarlett would like to organise the pony rides it had seemed like a good idea. Poppy had been obsessed with horses all her life and it wasn't so long ago that she would have happily traded the clothes on her back for five minutes on someone else's pony. It would be good to let other pony-mad kids have a ride on Cloud. She and Scarlett would have a laugh. But running the pony rides on her own wasn't going to be half as much fun.

She tied Cloud and Chester to the fence behind their car and gave them the haynets she'd filled earlier. Satisfied they were happy chomping away, she helped Caroline put the finishing touches to their stall.

"Have you decided who you're raising money for yet?" Caroline asked.

"Either the PTA or Charlie's tent fund, I suppose," she said, although she had little interest in either. She'd never attended Waterby Primary as they'd moved to Dartmoor when she was eleven. Her old primary school was miles away in Twickenham. And she would rather pull out her own fingernails one by one than join Charlie and his fellow Cubs for a night under canvas, even if the tent didn't leak.

She gave the handle of the tombola drum a hefty crank, imagining all the folded raffle tickets somersaulting inside like popcorn in a microwave. Her gaze wandered to the empty space next to their stall.

"Who's supposed to be there?"

"Some animal rescue charity, according to Pat." Caroline checked her watch. "But they need to get a shift on. The fete opens in fifteen minutes."

As she spoke an ancient Land Rover came flying into the field. It narrowly missed the Methodist ladies' cake stand and drove straight over a couple of the guy ropes on the bunting-clad tea tent. It finally came to an abrupt halt in front of the McKeevers' stall. A blonde girl in her early twenties in cut-off denim shorts and a red tee-shirt leapt out and slammed the door shut behind her.

"Is that for me?" she said without preamble, pointing to the space beside them.

Caroline stepped forward, a smile on her face. "Yes. Do you need a hand setting up? Poppy and I can help, can't we Poppy?"

Poppy, who had picked up a box of after dinner mints and was pretending to read the list of ingredients, shot her stepmother a mutinous look. "I need to go and get ready."

"Nonsense. You can spare ten minutes."

Inside the back of the Land Rover was a long trestle table and several tall display panels.

"Pat said you're from an animal rescue charity," said Caroline.

"Nethercote Horse Rescue," corrected the girl, pointing at the logo on her tee-shirt.

"We'll help you unload," Caroline told her. But the girl shook her head.

"I can manage."

Ignoring her, Caroline nodded to Poppy to take one end of the top display panel. As they opened it up Poppy almost dropped it in shock. A huge photograph pinned to the royal blue panel showed a skeletal skewbald mare. She was so thin Poppy could count every rib. Her sunken flanks were covered in angry red sores, her head drooped listlessly and her eyes were dull. She looked hours away from death.

"That's Kirsty. She was skin and bone when she came to us. She was riddled with worms and had infections in both her eyes. Our vet said she'd never pull through." The blonde girl's voice was matter-of-fact. She opened another fold of the display panel. "That photo was taken last week."

Poppy shook her head. She couldn't believe the plump mare standing proudly in a field, her skewbald coat glossy and her eyes bright with life, was the same horse.

"That's incredible."

The girl dipped her head in acknowledgement. "I think so."

Charlie appeared, his face painted like a Ninja warrior, the woollen donkey tail clutched in his hand. He looked the blonde girl up and down. "Who are you?"

"Jodie Morgan. Who are you?"

"Charlie McKeever. And that's my sister Poppy. But be very careful. She got out of bed the wrong side this morning."

Poppy glared at Charlie, who raced back out of their gazebo holding the tail in the air like a pennant. Sometimes he was so embarrassing.

She helped Jodie unload the rest of the panels. Before and after photos of horses and ponies were pinned to each section, with handwritten stories alongside each one. In one of the pictures a horse had overgrown hooves so long they curled up like Aladdin's slippers. Others had matted coats, hollow necks and bony rumps. Poppy had a sick feeling in the pit of her stomach. How could anyone treat an animal so badly? It was beyond belief.

"Some people complain our photos are too graphic and say we shouldn't use them because they upset people." Jodie gave a derisory snort. "I don't care. You can't sweep cruelty and neglect under the carpet. These pictures need to be seen. What do you think?"

Taken aback by her directness, Poppy glanced towards Caroline. But her stepmum was deep in conversation with the woman running the face-painting stand.

"They are shocking," she said. "But I agree with you. People should know it goes on. And maybe it'll help with donations."

Jodie's lips thinned. "If only. People have absolutely no idea how much it costs to run Nethercote. They seem to think I can feed the horses on thin air."

Charlie re-appeared. "It's one minute to ten, Poppy!" he cried. "You need to start the pony rides."

"Pony rides?" Jodie asked.

"My pony Cloud is over there with our donkey Chester."

Chester's long brown ears had flopped forward as he dozed but Cloud was looking around with interest as fete-goers began streaming into the field.

"Did you say Cloud?" Jodie said.

Poppy nodded, wondering why the older girl was staring at the Connemara as if she'd seen a ghost. Then she had an idea. "I was going to raise money for new tents but I'd much rather give the money to help your horses. It might not be much, but anything is better than nothing, right?"

Jodie dragged her eyes away from Cloud. "Yes," she echoed faintly. "Anything is better than nothing."

The next two hours passed in a blur of shortening

and lengthening stirrup leathers, giving leg-ups and leading young riders up and down the length of the field as proud parents snapped away on their mobile phones. Poppy had been worried how Cloud would react to the swarms of people but he was basking in all the attention, standing patiently as he was stroked and petted, taking the Polos and tufts of grass proffered on countless sticky palms so gently that Poppy's heart swelled with love. Chester was an old hand at village events and when Poppy hit on the idea of charging fifty pence for the privilege of having a selfie with the donkey an orderly queue quickly formed.

Halfway through the morning Jodie appeared with a plastic cup of lukewarm orange squash.

"Your mum sent me over with a drink. And you can put this on if you like," Jodie said, handing Poppy a red tee-shirt that matched her own.

Poppy pulled the tee-shirt over her head and smiled. "I reckon I've made about fifty pounds already."

"Wish I could say the same. People are so tight they won't even fork out the price of a cup of coffee." Jodie rubbed Cloud's forehead and he snuffled at the pocket of her shorts. She looked as if she was about to say something else, then thought better of it. She patted him on the neck and smiled briefly at Poppy. "Anyway, gotta go."

By two o'clock the queue of children waiting for a ride had dwindled to nothing. Poppy left Cloud tied up next to Chester and went in search of Caroline. Charlie charged through the crowd towards her, shaking an old biscuit tin heavy with loose change.

"I've made millions!" he said. "Enough to buy ten tents, I reckon."

"I've made lots, too. I was going to have a count up and give the money to Jodie before I take Cloud and Chester home."

"She's gone."

"You're joking."

"Nope. She told us it was a waste of time and she'd have been better off staying at home."

Poppy jiggled the coins in her pocket. "How am I supposed to get all this money to her?"

Charlie shrugged. "Ask Mum."

Poppy found Caroline at their stall wrestling with the trestle table.

"I was just about to come and find you. Are you all done?"

"Done in, more like. I'm shattered. You have no idea how tiring giving pony rides is." Poppy collapsed on the ground. "And Charlie said Jodie's already gone."

"She had to get back for the horses. I said we'd drive over tomorrow. There's a map on the back of the leaflet she was giving out." Caroline pulled a crumpled piece of paper from the pocket of her jeans. On the front was a picture of Kirsty the pretty skewbald mare looking inquisitively over her stable door. Inside were some of the before and after photos Jodie had used on her display board and on the back of the leaflet was a map.

"It's really close," Poppy said, surprised. Nethercote was half way between Waterby and Princetown. In fact she and Cloud must have ridden pretty close the day before. And yet until today she'd had no idea the horse rescue sanctuary even existed.

CHAPTER 3

The sanctuary was at the end of a long and windy track flanked by fields of black-faced sheep. Nethercote itself was a squat stone farmhouse with a slate roof and incongruously tall chimneys. Ivy crept up the walls and net curtains blocked the view into every window, giving the house a shuttered look. As Caroline parked the car Poppy noticed a small sign pointing around the side of the house.

"It says the rescue centre is this way."

Poppy led Caroline and Charlie through a gate and into a wide strip of concrete sandwiched between two long rows of whitewashed stables that looked as if they had once been cow byres. On the wall by a door to what Poppy presumed was the feed room was a bell with a sign above, *Please ring for attention.* She gave the bell pull a tentative tug and jumped a foot in the air when Jodie appeared over the nearest stable door and barked, "Who is it?"

"Only us," Caroline said.

The scowl on the older girl's face lifted fractionally.

"Sorry," she said, pushing the stable door open. "People think that because we're an animal sanctuary they have the right to just turn up on the doorstep any time they like."

Poppy fingered the small brown envelope in her pocket. "We've brought the money we raised yesterday," she said.

Jodie wiped her hands on her shorts. "Thanks."

Charlie, who had been walking up the line of empty stables peering into each one, fixed his cerulean blue eyes on Jodie and said, "Can we have a tour?"

Caroline smiled apologetically. "I'm sorry about my son. He has no manners. We can see you're busy. Perhaps we'll pop by another day."

Jodie checked her watch. "No, you're OK. I've got time to give you a quick tour. Show you where your money will go."

"I'd love to meet Kirsty," Poppy said shyly.

"Kirsty's gone, I'm afraid," Jodie said.

"Oh, no! What happened to her?"

"Not *gone* gone. I mean gone from here. She was put up for adoption in the spring. She's gone to live with a family near Taunton. She's settled in really well."

"That's good," Poppy said, relieved that the skewbald mare was still enjoying life after the cruelty and neglect she'd endured.

"We run an adoption scheme, otherwise we'd never be able to take on any more horses," Jodie said.

"How does that work?" Charlie asked, looking around with interest.

Caroline sighed. "Don't get any ideas, Charlie. We haven't got room for any more animals."

"I was just asking," Charlie said indignantly, then flashed a grin at Jodie. "We've already rescued our dog Freddie. We gave Chester a home when Tory couldn't look after him any more. And I suppose we sort of rescued Cloud. Dad says Riverdale's turning into a home for waifs and strays."

Jodie finally smiled. "Good for you. Why buy an animal when so many desperately need new homes?" She beckoned them to follow her to the fields at the end of the two rows of stables, where more than a dozen horses and ponies grazed, dozed in the sun or stood head to tail, swishing flies.

"Once a horse or pony has fully recovered they go up for adoption and I put their details on our website. New homes are vetted and if everything is OK they have the horse on permanent loan, with the understanding that should the horse need to come back for any reason, they'll always have a place at Nethercote."

Poppy gazed at the horses. An idea was forming in her mind. "Who's up for adoption at the moment," she asked.

"Percy. He's the Welsh Section A over there," said Jodie, pointing to a cheeky-looking grey gelding with a bushy mane and a pink nose. "He's available as a companion. And Mr Darcy. I called him that because he's tall, dark and handsome." They followed Jodie's gaze to a dark bay thoroughbred gelding who was grazing next to a swaybacked chestnut mare. "He has a touch of arthritis so can only do light work."

"You haven't got any between fourteen and fifteen hands?" Poppy said hopefully.

Charlie gaped at her. "You don't need another pony. You've got Cloud!"

"Not for me, you twit. I was thinking of Scarlett. She's my best friend," Poppy explained, ignoring the fact that Scarlett hadn't spoken to her for a whole forty eight hours, the longest time they'd ever fallen out. "She lives on the farm next door to us. She's almost outgrown her pony but her parents can't afford to buy her a new one. I was wondering if you had anything that she could adopt."

Jodie leant on the fence and stared at her disparate herd of horses and ponies. "Is she a good rider?"

"Really good. She's been riding since she was two."

"She lives on a farm, you say?"

Poppy nodded. "They've got loads of lovely grazing and a spare stable and whoever came would have two Dartmoor ponies for company."

"There is someone who might fit the bill."

Jodie whistled and a rangy chestnut gelding lifted his head and trotted over. He gave Jodie a gentle butt and she scratched his ear affectionately.

"This is Red. He was born at Nethercote. We didn't realise his dam was in foal at first. Unfortunately we lost her the night he was born and I had to hand rear him. I started breaking him this spring. He's coming on well but he needs to go to a really experienced home."

Poppy knew Scarlett would fall in love with the chestnut gelding the minute she saw him. He was a couple of inches bigger than Cloud and had a flaxen mane and tail, four white socks, an extra daub of white on his nose and kind eyes. Poppy imagined Red and Cloud cantering along a moorland track together, matching each other stride for stride. He was absolutely perfect.

"She would have to come and see him first," said Jodie. "I only let horses go if I'm satisfied they are a good match with their new guardian."

"That won't be a problem," Poppy said. "I'll speak to her when I get home."

"Do you get upset when the horses go to their new homes?" Charlie asked.

"Can't afford to. A job like this toughens you up."

"He's sweet," said Caroline, pointing to an appaloosa pony who was lying down in the sun.

"He looks like he's been out in a snowstorm," said Charlie.

He was right, Poppy thought. The white spots on the pony's chestnut back looked like snowflakes.

"That's Biscuit. All the horses here have a story to tell, but his is probably the most incredible. If you read about it in a book you wouldn't believe it," said Jodie. "He was found by the RSPCA tethered to railings on top of a tower block of flats in the Midlands."

"I remember that!" Caroline said. "I saw it on the news. They had to airlift him down by helicopter, didn't they?"

"That's right. The lift was broken and they thought it would be less traumatic for him to be winched down by helicopter than to be carried down the twenty seven flights of stairs."

Charlie was staring at Biscuit with his mouth open. "He lived on top of the building?"

Jodie nodded. "No-one knows for sure how long he'd been up there. And no-one was ever prosecuted. Neither the RSPCA nor the police could prove who he belonged to. He'd been kept alive on vegetable peelings, scraps of bread and rainwater. He was pretty thin and had terrible rain scald when he came to us."

Poppy couldn't imagine what life must have been like for Biscuit, living on his own on top of a tower block, with sheer drops in every direction, at the mercy of the elements.

"That's awful. How was he found?"

"A new tenant moved in and tipped off the RSPCA. The inspector told me their call centre didn't believe him at first and they almost dismissed it as a prank call. Luckily for Biscuit someone decided to check it out."

"He looks pretty content now," said Caroline. Biscuit yawned, showing a row of yellow teeth, and collapsed, asleep, in the daisies.

Jodie smiled. "He is the most chilled out pony I have ever known. Sometimes, when things get on top of me and I fantasise about walking away from it all, I look at Biscuit and remember what all the blood, sweat and tears are for. He keeps me going."

"Do you run the centre on your own?" Poppy asked.

Jodie gazed at Biscuit's snowflake-splotched flanks gently rising and falling. Poppy was shocked to see a look of bitterness darken her features, but the expression was so fleeting she wondered if she'd imagined it.

"This is my dad's dream, not mine," Jodie said eventually.

"So he helps you with the horses?"

"He would if he could," Jodie conceded. "But he's away at the moment."

"Our dad's always away, too. He works for the BBC," said Charlie. "What does your dad do?"

Jodie bent down to pick a handful of grass for a bay mare who had wandered over to say hello. "He runs a small import business. Mobile phones, mainly."

Caroline looked impressed. "Mobiles are big

business. He must be doing well."

"Not really. It's a very confined market where he is. In more ways than one," she muttered.

Poppy remembered the envelope in her pocket.

"Here's the money we made yesterday. I hope it helps a little bit."

The older girl gave the ghost of a smile. "It'll keep the wolf from the door for a few days."

CHAPTER 4

Caroline had barely pulled up the handbrake before Poppy had unclipped her seatbelt and jumped out of the passenger door.

"I'm going to tell Scarlett about Red," Poppy said.

She'd taken a dozen photos of the chestnut gelding on her phone and scrolled through them as she crossed the field of sheep that separated Riverdale and Ashworthy, the farm where Scarlett lived with her older brother Alex and their parents Bill and Pat. Red was the same shade of burnt umber as both Blaze and Scarlett's own auburn hair. It was fate, Poppy told herself, as she climbed over the gate onto the roughshod Ashworthy drive. All she had to do was convince Scarlett to see her.

Pat was kneading a huge ball of dough in the farm's shabby but cosy kitchen when Poppy poked her head around the door.

"I wondered if Scarlett wanted some company."

Pat pushed the dough down and out with the heel of her hand, pulled it back into a ball and sprinkled it with flour. She nodded in the direction of the lounge. "Your guess is as good as mine. She's been moping around the house since Friday. I don't know what's up with her."

"Caroline said she wasn't very well and that's why she didn't come to the fete yesterday."

Pat dropped the dough into a bowl to prove on top of the Rayburn. "That's what she says, but I'm not convinced. She hasn't got a temperature. She hasn't been sick. She just seems to be down in the dumps. Perhaps you can cheer her up."

"I'll do my best. But before I do, can I talk to you about something?"

Poppy took a deep breath and pushed open the door to the lounge. Scarlett, wearing faded My Little Pony pyjamas and a glowering expression, was curled up on the sofa with Meg, the family's border collie. The dog gave a welcoming woof and jumped down to see Poppy, her tail wagging.

"At least someone's pleased to see me," joked Poppy. She stroked Meg's silky ears and chanced another look at Scarlett. On closer inspection she realised her best friend was clutching a tissue and her eyes were red-rimmed.

"Hey, are you OK?"

Scarlett waved the remote control at the television. They watched together as a beautiful bay gelding galloped in blind panic through No Man's Land, shells exploding all around him and barbed wire tearing his chest. War Horse was one of Poppy's all-time favourite films - it was right up there with International Velvet - but it was so sad it was enough to make a statue weep. No wonder Scarlett was crying.

"Turn it off before Joey gets caught in the barbed wire. I can't stand that bit," Poppy said, plonking herself down on the sofa beside Scarlett. "I know you're really cross with me, and I don't blame you, but I've got some really exciting news I promise you'll want to hear."

Scarlett blew her noise noisily and glared at Poppy, who ignored her and reached in her back pocket for her phone.

"This is Red. He's fifteen hands and four years old. Gorgeous, isn't he?"

Scarlett glanced at the screen and looked away. "Are you getting another horse?" she said dully.

"No, you idiot, he's for you!"

A damson-dark flush was inching its way up Scarlett's neck. "How many times do I have to spell it out, Poppy? Mum and Dad can't afford another horse."

"Red's not for sale."

"So why are you showing me his picture?" Scarlett uncurled her legs and swung her feet to the floor. "I'm going upstairs."

"Blimey, Scarlett, you can be a stroppy mare sometimes. Just listen for a minute, will you? Red is a rescue horse. He lives at Nethercote Horse Rescue. He's about to go up for adoption. I've had a word with the girl who runs the place. He's as good as yours if you pass the home visit and you and he get on."

Eyes wide, Scarlett gawped at Poppy. "Are you serious?"

"Absolutely. We met Jodie, the girl who runs the rescue centre, at the fete yesterday. She's -"

But Scarlett wasn't listening. She was two steps ahead and her voice was resigned. "It won't work. Mum and Dad are bound to say no. It's another mouth to feed, isn't it? Another horse to shoe. More vet's bills. Tack we can't afford."

The door opened and Pat appeared with two mugs of tea. "What can't we afford?" she asked, winking at Poppy.

"Nothing," said Scarlett, sliding Poppy's phone down the side of the sofa.

"Poppy's just been showing me the photos of Red. He's a handsome lad, isn't he?" Pat set the mugs on the coffee table. "Are you going to go and see him?"

"There's no point, is there? We can't afford to keep him."

Pat smiled at her daughter. "Barney was only asking me the other day if you might be interested in a Saturday job at the shop. If you take him up on his offer and use your wages towards Red's keep, I'll make sure we find the rest. It's been a good year for lambing and the pigs are doing really well. You'll have to make do with second-hand tack, but you're used to hand-me-downs, aren't you?"

Scarlett nodded, a smile creeping across her freckled face at last. She sprang up from the sofa and threw her arms around her mum.

"You have Poppy to thank. It was all her idea," Pat said.

Poppy caught Scarlett's eye. "Am I forgiven?"

Scarlett's forehead creased in a frown and she tilted her head to one side and rubbed her chin thoughtfully. Poppy's heart sank. If finding Scarlett a new horse wasn't enough to win her over she didn't know what was. Then Scarlett broke free from her

THE SECRET OF WITCH COTTAGE

"Of course you are, you twit! I had already forgiven you really. I should know by now that tact isn't one of your strong points. I was just feeling sorry for myself. And now I feel like Christmas has come early and Santa has promised me the best present ever!"

Friends again, the two girls celebrated with a ride. Feeling magnanimous, Poppy asked Charlie if he wanted to tag along on his bike. "As long as you only speak when spoken to and promise not to be annoying," she told him sternly.

Charlie smiled his sweetest smile. "I'm *never* annoying."

"Ha! That's open for debate."

Back at Ashworthy Scarlett was zinging with excitement. "Mum's phoned Jodie. We're going to see Red in the morning. Want to come, too?"

"You bet."

"Never mind tomorrow. Where are we going today?" Charlie asked.

"Follow me," Poppy said mysteriously. "I know exactly where I want to go."

Cloud's ears were pricked as they approached the band of conifers that cloaked the tumbledown cottage. The ground was so squelchy Charlie had to push his mountain bike. "My feet are soaking," he grumbled. "Where exactly are we supposed to be going?"

"Stop whingeing and keep walking, little brother. It's worth the wait, I promise."

They plunged into the conifers. Poppy grinned at the other two. "Almost there."

Scarlett gasped when she saw the dilapidated

29

building and the dark waters of the tarn.

"It's Witch Cottage! We can't go there!"

Poppy jumped off Cloud and gave Scarlett a puzzled look.

"It's fine. Cloud and I explored it the other day. No-one lives there any more. I reckon it's been empty for years."

"You don't understand! It's haunted!"

Charlie propped his bike against a tree and stared at Scarlett agog.

"The pool's in the shape of a tear, isn't it?" Scarlett said.

Poppy nodded. "Why?"

"My Granny Martha used to say the pool came from a single teardrop wept by an old woman whose only son was killed in a tin mining accident like about five hundred years ago. Granny said it's bottomless, and anyone who gazes into the waters at midnight on Midsummer's Eve will see a reflection of the next person in the parish to die."

Scarlett's voice had taken on a low, chilling tone. "People thought the old crone was a witch and one full moon a group of villagers crept into her cottage, dragged her from her bed and burnt her and her familiar at the stake."

Charlie frowned. "Her familiar what?"

"A familiar is another name for a witch's animal companion, Charlie. In this case it was a cat."

Poppy tutted. What a cliché. "Was it black, by any chance?"

"No, it was ginger, actually. He was called Marmaduke. That's what the legend says, anyway. And now the witch can be seen gliding around the banks of the pool on the night of every full moon, with Marmaduke riding on her withered old shoulders and the ends of her tattered cloak on fire."

By this time they had reached the stone wall surrounding the cottage and tarn.

"*And*," said Scarlett, pointing to a small wooden cross Poppy hadn't noticed before. "About five years ago a group of wild swimmers were crossing the pool when one of them got into difficulties and drowned. And do you know what?"

"What?" breathed Charlie, who was hanging onto her every word.

"The swimmer who died was *exactly* the same age as the old woman's son when he was killed in the tin mine." Scarlett drew her hand across her neck in a cut-throat gesture. Poppy rolled her eyes.

"But that's not all," Scarlett said dramatically. "Sometimes at night lights can be seen in the windows of the cottage. Some people say it's the old crone lighting candles in memory of her son."

"Some people talk a load of absolute rubbish," said Poppy. "Are you going to come and have a look around or what?"

Scarlett was aghast. "Haven't you heard a word of what I've been saying? There's no way you're dragging me into that house of horrors. I'll stay and look after the ponies, thanks."

Charlie had no such reservations. He sprinted to the crooked front door and heaved it open, beckoning Poppy to follow. She handed Cloud's reins to Scarlett and ran after him.

Charlie was already disappearing up the creaky staircase.

"Be careful, some of the floorboards are a bit rotten," she called.

"No need to worry, sis. I can look after myself," he shouted back.

"Famous last words," Poppy muttered, inspecting the decrepit remains of the kitchen. Someone must have lived in the cottage since the old crone in Scarlett's dubious legend, although Poppy guessed the house must have been empty for at least half a century. A corroded black kettle sat atop the rusty range. A couple of tarnished knives and forks gathered dust on some woodworm-infested shelves. Poppy pulled open a couple of cupboards, but there was nothing inside apart from ancient cobwebs and a couple of dead bluebottles. Upstairs she could hear Charlie exclaiming with delight as he thundered between the two bedrooms like a baby elephant with a sugar rush.

She was prising open the door of the range when there was a shout and the ceiling above her head shook ominously, sprinkling her with a layer of dust as fine as icing sugar. She raced up the stairs, two at a time. Charlie was sitting with his back to her, hugging his right knee.

"What on earth's happened?"

Charlie looked over his shoulder. "My foot's stuck," he said sheepishly.

"In one of those rotten floorboards I warned you about?" Poppy knelt down next to him. Charlie's foot had broken clean-through the crumbling plank and was wedged between two joists. She slipped her hand into the gap and felt for his shoe. "I think it's your trainer that's stuck. If I undo your laces you should be able to wiggle your foot out. We'll give it a try."

Poppy began picking at the double knot but the gap was so small that every time she moved her hand she grazed her knuckles on the rough underside of the floorboards. Eventually she felt the laces slither undone. She sat back on her haunches and Charlie wiggled out his foot.

"You're lucky you didn't break your ankle," Poppy told him, reaching back into the gap for his trainer. As she did her fingers brushed against a hard edge. It didn't feel like a joist. It was more like the cover of a book. Poppy leant on her elbows and slid her hand further in. It was definitely a book. But who would hide a book beneath the floorboards of an abandoned croft where an old woman who may or may not have been a witch had once lived? The hairs on the back of her neck stood up.

"Have you got my shoe yet?" Charlie asked. He had a cobweb in his hair and his knees were filthy.

"No, it's caught on something" she lied, keen to keep this discovery to herself. "Go over to the window. There's a swallow's nest under the eaves. See if you can see the babies."

Once Poppy was sure his attention was diverted she swivelled around on her heels so her back was facing him and pulled out the book. It was long and slim with a black cover and the year embossed in silver leaf on the front. A diary. Poppy flicked through it, as furtive as a pickpocket stealing a wallet. Pages and pages were crammed with tiny writing. Her heart was hammering in her ribcage as she tried to decipher the loops and curls.

"What are you doing?" Charlie asked.

"Nothing," said Poppy, tucking the diary in her waistband and reaching back into the hole in the floorboards. "Here's your shoe," she said, tossing him the white and navy trainer. She checked her watch.

"We'd better go or Scarlett will have a fit. She hates it here."

"I think it's awesome. It could be our secret den where we plan all our adventures."

"Maybe we'll come over on the next full moon. See if Scarlett's right about the place being haunted," said Poppy, half-joking.

But if she thought her brother would be fazed by any ghostly goings-on she was wrong. His eyes were sparkling.

"Cool idea!" he said, grinning at Poppy. "Why didn't I think of that?"

The diary pressed uncomfortably into Poppy's back all the way home. As they cantered across the moor, Charlie pedalling furiously to keep up, she wondered why she hadn't shared her discovery with Scarlett. Perhaps it was because her best friend had showed no desire to have anything to do with the tumbledown cottage. She'd flung Cloud's reins at Poppy and jumped on Blaze the second they'd re-appeared, muttering about bad vibes and negative energy. Scarlett was one of the most superstitious people Poppy knew. She shrieked with horror if Poppy spilled salt and forgot to hurl a pinch of it over her left shoulder, and if Poppy dared dice with death by walking under a ladder she virtually went into meltdown. Poppy didn't hold any truck with superstitions - she supposed it was having a cynical journalist as a dad. As far as she was concerned Scarlett's tale of supernatural happenings was utter nonsense.

"We're leaving at ten tomorrow," Scarlett said, as they clip-clopped down the Ashworthy drive.

"I'll be there," Poppy said, grimacing as she surreptitiously shifted the diary further down her jodhpurs.

"Why are you pulling a face? Don't you want to come?"

"'Course I do. I'm just trying to scratch a mosquito bite," Poppy lied.

Back home, once she'd turned Cloud out with Chester, Poppy raced upstairs to her bedroom, closed the door, and propped her old wicker chair under the door handle. It wouldn't stop Charlie coming in, but it would buy her enough time to hide her find. She sat cross-legged on her bed and opened the diary with trembling fingers.

CHAPTER 5

The first two pages were covered in doodles. Circles and spirals, squares and triangles, stars and flowers. So many squiggles and scribbles that at first Poppy didn't see the three words in the middle of the facing page. When she did, she blinked and looked again, in case the loopy, slanting script somehow untangled itself and snaked into three completely different words. It didn't. The words were there in black and white. *Caitlyn Jones's Diary.*

Poppy realised she was gripping the book so tightly she was in danger of breaking the spine. She closed it, drummed her fingers on the black leather cover and wondered what to do. Caitlyn Jones had always been a complete enigma to Poppy. Someone she had obsessed about and felt inferior to ever since the McKeevers had moved to Riverdale. Someone who, if ghosts did actually exist, came as close to haunting Poppy's subconscious as anyone ever would.

Caitlyn was the other girl in Cloud's life. Poppy corrected herself. *Had been* the other girl in his life.

Not any more.

There was a photo of Caitlyn and Cloud in Tory's flat, taken at the Brambleton Horse Show the same year Poppy's mum Isobel died. Poppy scrutinised it every time she visited, battling the jealousy and inadequacy it inevitably stirred, feelings that were as invasive as goosegrass, no matter how hard she tried to suppress them.

Poppy loved Cloud with all her heart. She would walk over burning coals for him, no question. And she knew her pony loved her. After all, he'd found her when he'd been let loose on the moor during their stay at Redhall Manor Equestrian Centre, hadn't he? But did he love her as much as he'd loved Caitlyn? Poppy had no answer to that.

And yet here, in her hands, was the key to unlock Caitlyn's innermost thoughts. A window to her dreams and fears. A chance for Poppy to see the world through Cait's eyes.

Poppy gazed at the diary almost reverently, her fingers flicking through the pages as if it was a kids' flip book. She itched to read it. And yet the diary held secrets and thoughts Caitlyn had scribbled down never imagining that anyone else would ever see them. It was private property. Poppy had kept a diary ever since Caroline had bought her one for Christmas the previous year. She hated the thought of anyone reading it. It would be so embarrassing. More than that, it would make her feel exposed, vulnerable. Poppy slammed the book shut. If she felt like that about her own diary, it would be hypocritical for her to read someone else's, wouldn't it?

Poppy shoved the diary under her pillow and stood up. She was halfway across her room when she stopped, as if glued to the floor. The desire to read the diary was overwhelming. Caitlyn was dead, killed seven years ago when Cloud fell at a fence during a hunter trial. What harm could reading it do? Poppy would never divulge what she'd read. It would be their secret, a bond between them as strong as the one they each shared with Cloud. With a certainty she couldn't explain, Poppy knew Caitlyn wouldn't mind. She spun on her heels, jumped back on her bed and pulled out the diary before she could change her mind.

A slip of folded paper fluttered out of the pages and settled between her crossed legs like a sycamore seed on a blustery autumn day. It was an old newspaper cutting, brittle and flaking. Poppy smoothed it out, tucked a strand of hair behind her ear and began to read.

Friends and rivals compete for showjumping glory

Best friends Jodie Morgan and Caitlyn Jones were the only two young riders to make it through to the jump-off in the final class at the South Devon Open Showjumping Competition on Saturday.
Fourteen-year-old Jodie and her pony Nethercote Nero jumped first, giving a textbook performance with a fast, clean round, piling on the pressure for her thirteen-year-old friend and fellow Pony Club showjumping team member Caitlyn.
Caitlyn and her pony Cloud Nine looked like they were in with a chance, but knocked a pole in the double to collect four faults and second place.
Earlier this year Jodie, a rising showjumping talent,

was selected to represent Great Britain in the British Showjumping Pony European Championships squad. "Both Nero and Cloud have been jumping out of their skin all season so winning the open jumping class against such stiff competition was pretty special," said Jodie.

"Hopefully we can keep up the momentum for the European Championships in Malmo, Sweden, in August."

Jodie and Caitlyn had been best friends! Poppy studied the photo next to the story, the diary forgotten. Cloud stood proudly, his neck arched and his mane neatly plaited, an enormous blue rosette fixed to his browband. Caitlyn sat gracefully astride him, holding the reins with one hand, her head turned towards the girl next to her, who was riding an eye-catching light bay gelding, her hand clasped around the stem of a silver trophy. Jodie was winking at Caitlyn and laughing. She looked younger, more carefree, less spiky, but it was definitely her. Poppy checked the date. Seven years ago. She squinted at Nero, trying to remember if she'd seen him when they'd visited Nethercote. She didn't think so. She was sure she'd have remembered him.

Poppy supposed it was no fluke that the two girls had known each other. They must have been in the same school year and they were both talented riders. They had a lot in common. It was inevitable they'd been friends. Suddenly Jodie's reaction to Cloud made sense. Poppy shivered. Poor Jodie. Coming face to face with her old friend's pony must have been a shock.

A thump, thump, thump on the stairs caught her

attention and the handle on her bedroom door turned. Poppy shoved the newspaper cutting back in the diary and slipped it under her mattress. She streaked across the room and whipped the wicker chair away as the door creaked and swung open.

Charlie eyed her suspiciously. "Why are you holding your chair?"

"Just re-arranging my room. Felt like a change," Poppy said airily.

Charlie raised his eyebrows. "Mum sent me up. Dinner's nearly ready. You need to come down and lay the table."

Poppy didn't get another chance to look at the diary until she'd gone to bed. Her lamp cast a pool of sallow light over the crackly pages as she scoured the tiny loopy handwriting, looking for mentions of Cloud. She found the first on the fifth of January.

Mum finally agreed to drive me up to Gran's this morning. I was getting desperate. I hadn't seen Cloud since New Year's Eve. That's five whole days ago! I think he was pleased to see me. But not as pleased as I was to see him! It was freezing, but we managed a quick ride around the lanes. I'm never going to get his fitness up for competing if I can only ride a couple of times a week. Gran said she would've lunged him but the fields were too waterlogged. But I shouldn't have to rely on her to exercise my pony. Mum just doesn't get it. I wish, wish, wish she was into horses like Jodie's dad is. She doesn't know how lucky she is.

Poppy realised she was lucky, too. Imagine only seeing Cloud a couple of times a week! It would be torture. She could see him first thing every morning and last thing at night. She could ride him whenever she wanted. She could even watch him from her bedroom window. They spent every spare second together. For the first time in her life Poppy felt stirrings of sympathy for Caitlyn.

She scanned through the weekday entries, which seemed to consist mainly of Caitlyn moaning about school and the amount of homework she'd been given. The bits that fascinated her were the references to Cloud and Jodie. One entry on the twentieth of May caught her attention.

What a fantastic weekend! The Annoying Parents had some boring wedding to go to in Somerset. They were going to take me until I suggested I stayed at Gran's. So they dropped me off at eight yesterday morning and didn't pick me up until six tonight. It was brilliant, having a whole two days with Cloud. And Chester and Gran of course. Jodie's dad brought Nero over in their box yesterday and we went on this amazingly long ride. We were gone for hours. Mum would have been panicking, thinking we'd been kidnapped by aliens or something, but Gran's so chilled. She always says she trusts Cloud to look after me. Anyway, we found this awesome place. It's an old abandoned cottage over towards Princetown way. You have to ride through a forest to reach it. There's even a small lake for the ponies to drink from. We decided we'd hang out there whenever we can. It's so cool.

And then a couple of weeks later:

No shows this weekend so Jodie and I rode over to the

cottage. We took a picnic this time, which we ate on the banks of the lake. I brought along an article I'd printed from the internet about how to teach your horse tricks. It was so funny. Honestly, we were in stitches. Cloud was a quick learner, and by the end of the afternoon he was giving me a kiss for a pony nut. Nero was hopeless. But secretly I didn't mind. It was nice to be better at something than Jodie for once!

Poppy yawned and checked the time. Five to eleven. She closed the diary, slid it back under her mattress and turned off her bedside lamp. It's funny, she thought sleepily, as she wiggled under the duvet trying to get comfortable. She'd spent two years feeling inferior to Caitlyn. But, as she'd flicked through pages and pages peppered with the insights and insecurities of any teenage girl, she realised they were not so very different after all.

CHAPTER 6

A fine drizzle as soft as a whisper had settled on the moor overnight and, despite promises by the weathermen that the afternoon would be hot and sunny, the mizzle seemed as stubborn to linger as an unwelcome houseguest reluctant to pack their bags and go home. Poppy's hair had frizzed by the time she had fed Cloud and Chester, cleaned and re-filled their water trough and poo-picked their field.

She was changing into a pair of marginally-cleaner jodhpurs when she heard the toot of a horn and saw Bill's Land Rover bump to a halt outside the front door. Scarlett slid across the bench seat to make room for her.

"Excited?" Poppy said, fixing her seatbelt.

"I feel a bit sick, actually."

Poppy was surprised. Scarlett usually took everything in her stride. Things that would make Poppy's knees knock with fear, like meeting new people or talking to the whole school during assembly, never fazed her. She was normally so confident and laidback, everything Poppy wasn't.

"What's up?"

Scarlett hugged herself. "What if Jodie takes one look at me and decides she hates me? What if Red and I don't click? What if we fail the home check? So many things could go wrong."

"It'll all be fine," Poppy soothed.

Scarlett stared glumly ahead as the windscreen wipers whisked to and fro, and remained unusually quiet as they trundled through the lanes to Nethercote. Poppy chatted to Bill about the fete, although her mind was elsewhere. She hadn't made up her mind whether or not to tell Jodie that she knew she and Caitlyn had been friends. She wanted to know if Jodie had ever made the European Championships in Sweden. According to the newspaper cutting she was a promising young rider. So why was she working her fingers to the bone at a small, local horse rescue centre in the middle of Dartmoor and not competing for glory on the national showjumping circuit? Poppy remembered a throwaway remark Jodie had made during their visit. She'd said the horse sanctuary was her dad's dream, not hers. Had her dream been to be a professional showjumper? If so, why had she thrown it all away to look after the rescue horses? And where was her dad in all of this? It didn't make sense.

Bill turned off the main road and the Land Rover lurched along the long and windy track to Nethercote. Poppy jumped out and pointed to the side of the house. "It's this way."

Scarlett and Bill followed her to the two long rows of whitewashed stables. A familiar spotted head appeared over the door of the nearest stable.

"Hello Biscuit." Poppy felt in her pocket for some pony nuts and offered them to the appaloosa. "He was rescued from a high rise block of flats," she told Scarlett, who was looking decidedly green.

But Scarlett wasn't listening. Her eyes were tracking back and forth across the yard. "Is there a loo?"

Poppy spied Jodie leading Red out of the paddock. The chestnut gelding walked obediently by her side. It wasn't until the pair reached them that Poppy realised he wasn't wearing a headcollar.

Jodie read her mind. "I don't bother with one. He's always followed me around like a shadow. It's because I hand-reared him."

Scarlett gazed at Red, her expression a jumble of longing and fear. She held out her hand tentatively and the gelding stretched his neck and blew gently into her palm. Scarlett scratched his poll and beamed at them. "He's the most beautiful horse I have ever seen in my life."

"I wouldn't go that far, but yes, he's not a bad sort," said Jodie.

Jodie tacked Red up and led him to the mounting block.

"He was only backed in the spring and is still very green, but he's a fast learner," she said, holding the gelding while Scarlett swung deftly into the saddle. Her hazel eyes were sparkling as she followed Jodie into a small, empty paddock.

"Have a walk and trot and see how he feels."

Poppy, Bill and Jodie leant on the post and rail fence and watched Scarlett and Red as they walked around the field.

"You're right, she's a nice little rider," Jodie said.

"Aye," said Bill. "She learnt as soon as she could

walk and hasn't stopped since. It's broken her heart that she's almost outgrown Blaze, especially as we couldn't afford to buy her another horse, but she's never once complained. She's a good girl, is our Scarlett, and she'll look after your Red, I promise you that."

There was a catch in Bill's normally gruff voice. Poppy caught Jodie's eye and was surprised to see her face darken.

"She's lucky to have a dad like you."

Red trotted past, his chestnut ears pricked. Jodie gave a brief smile. "I'll need to do a home visit of course, but I think we can safely say these two were a match made in heaven. The adoption forms are in the house. I'll go and find one."

Scarlett jumped off Red and smothered him with kisses. "I'm in love," she declared, and then clutched Poppy's arm. "Do you think I did OK?"

"More than OK. Jodie said you two were a match made in heaven. She's just gone to get the paperwork."

Scarlett flung her arms around the chestnut gelding's neck. Red seemed to be enjoying the attention. Poppy loosened his girth and ran up his stirrup leathers.

Bill checked his watch. "We'd better make a move. Baxters are delivering the pig feed in half an hour."

"Do you think we should turn Red out?" Scarlett asked.

"I don't know. I'll go and find Jodie." Poppy ran past the stables to the house. As she drew near to the open back door the sound of raised voices and the angry clatter of saucepans stopped her in her tracks.

A woman's voice, high-pitched, verging on hysterical, rang out. "I don't care what your father says. I don't want you to do it!"

"But it's not about what you or I want, is it? It never has been," Jodie hissed back.

"We'll manage somehow. I'll ask for some more shifts at the pub."

"A few extra hours' pulling pints won't feed this lot, Mum. You know that. I can make more in one night than you earn in a year."

"I'll sell my wedding ring. That'll give us a bit of breathing space while we work something out."

"Don't be ridiculous. It's the only piece of jewellery you have left."

"Do you think I care more about a band of gold than I care about you?" The woman's voice softened, and Poppy had to strain to hear her. "I worry, Jodie love. What happens if you get caught?"

Jodie laughed mirthlessly. "We'll end up with two black sheep in the family, won't we? But don't worry, it'll be fine. I've gone over it a million times. Nothing can go wrong."

Poppy darted back into the stable yard. She was scratching Biscuit's ear in what she hoped was a nonchalant manner when Jodie stalked out of the house, the adoption papers in one hand and a biro in the other.

"I see you've found a friend," Jodie remarked, pausing to stroke the appaloosa's speckled forehead.

Poppy reddened, even though there was no way Jodie could have known she'd eavesdropped. "We weren't sure what you wanted us to do with Red," she mumbled.

"We'll put him back in the field."

Poppy stole a look at the older girl as they walked across to Scarlett and Bill. There was a fierce expression on her face and a resolute set to her shoulders. Jodie caught her staring and raised her eyebrows.

"Anything wrong?" she asked.

I should be the one asking that, Poppy thought. Why was Jodie's mum so worried? What was it she didn't want Jodie to do? Instead she shook her head and smiled brightly.

"No. Everything is absolutely fine."

CHAPTER 7

The hands of Poppy's battered Mickey Mouse alarm clock had barely crawled around to seven o'clock the next morning when Charlie bounded into her bedroom.

"Don't forget our picnic! I've already planned our route and made some sandwiches. I just need to do drinks and some cake. It's going to be epic." Charlie bounced back out of the room. Poppy groaned. She'd planned to spend the day helping Scarlett clear out the old stable Bill had earmarked for Red. She'd forgotten she'd promised her brother that they'd spend the day on the moor. She couldn't pull out. She'd never hear the end of it. Sighing, she threw back the duvet, waking Magpie, the McKeevers' cat, who had been snoring softly at the end of her bed. He narrowed his emerald green eyes at her before tucking his head between his paws and going back to sleep. Poppy reached for her mobile and texted Scarlett to say she would try and pop round before dinner.

Downstairs, Charlie was carefully cutting squares of

lemon drizzle cake and wrapping them in cling film.

"I've cut up some carrots for Cloud. I even peeled them for him," he said. Caroline had only recently let Charlie start using the sharp kitchen knives. Personally Poppy thought it was asking for trouble and quite expected to find pieces of chopped finger in her food, but by some small miracle he had so far managed to keep all his digits intact.

"Where d'you want to go?" she asked.

"I thought we'd try somewhere new."

Poppy was surprised. Usually they picnicked in the Riverdale wood, on the small sandy strip of beach where they'd first seen Cloud. And then the penny dropped.

"Are we going to the old cottage by any chance?"

"What old cottage?" said Caroline, walking into the kitchen with a basket of dirty laundry balanced on her hip.

Charlie held his finger to his lips and Poppy nodded. She was as keen to go back to the old croft as her brother but knew that Caroline would worry if she knew. Deep water and derelict buildings seemed to freak adults out.

"Charlie wants to head down the bridleway that goes past the thatched cottage by the church," Poppy said, crossing her fingers behind her back.

"Sounds lovely. I wish I could come too, but I must do some gardening. Make sure you've got your phone with you, and be back by four at the latest. Otherwise I'll send out a search party."

"And we don't want that happening again, do we?" said Poppy, remembering the day she and Charlie had had to be rescued from the moor the first summer they'd moved to Riverdale.

"We certainly don't!" Caroline said, giving her a hug.

Poppy split their picnic into the two small saddle bags resting on Cloud's dappled grey flanks and tightened his girth. Smelling the carrots, the Connemara nibbled the hem of her checked shirt. She blew into his nose and he blew softly back.

"Ready?" she called to Charlie, who was wheeling his bike out of the barn. He was wearing a cycling helmet, a pair of their dad's old aviator sunglasses and his school rucksack.

"You bet!"

Poppy jumped into the saddle. "Come on then, let's have ourselves an adventure!"

The August sun was high in the sky as they let themselves out of the gate that led to the moor. Puffs of candyfloss cloud wafted by and in the distance three crows shamelessly mobbed a buzzard. Soon they had left Waterby behind and were climbing steadily towards Princetown. The wind ruffled Cloud's mane as he tossed his head and snatched at the bit.

"OK for a canter?" she asked. Charlie nodded. He crouched low over the handlebars and started pedalling furiously, his elbows jutting out like chicken wings. Poppy kicked Cloud on, keeping pace with her brother until she could see he was beginning to tire.

Before long the dark green belt of conifers appeared on the horizon.

"Those trees are the perfect camouflage, hiding Witch Cottage from prying eyes and nosy parkers," Charlie said.

"I'd never have found it if it wasn't for Cloud," Poppy agreed.

"Do you think he'd been there before?"

Poppy pictured Caitlyn's diary, hidden in the bottom of her sock drawer. "Maybe," she hedged, as they wound their way through the evergreens.

Charlie flung his bike and rucksack on the grass and raced over to the tumbledown building. Poppy watched him pull open the front door and disappear inside. Seconds later a startled pigeon flew out of the hole in the roof in a blur of feathers and affront. Poppy jumped off Cloud and led him over to the banks of the tarn. She stared at their reflections as he drank, remembering Scarlett's ghost stories about the old woman and her son and the superstition that claimed anyone gazing into the still waters on Midsummer's Eve would see a reflection of the next person in the parish to die.

"Utter rubbish," Poppy told her undulating reflection. A second face appeared at her side and she shrieked.

"Charlie! Don't creep up on me like that! You nearly gave me a heart attack!"

"Thought you didn't believe in ghosts," he grinned.

"I don't, you twit. You made me jump, that's all."

"If you say so," Charlie said, undoing the saddle bags. Poppy ran up her stirrups and loosened Cloud's girth. Looping his reins over the crook of her arm she sat cross-legged at the water's edge and caught the crumpled bag of crisps Charlie lobbed her way.

"Chocolate spread and cheese?" he asked, holding out a squashed-looking sandwich.

"Don't you mean chocolate spread *or* cheese?"

Charlie shook his head. "Nope. Chocolate spread *and* cheese. I was going to make jam and ham, it had a nice ring to it, but I thought it might be a bit *out there* for you." He gave her a faintly patronising look, as if she was an aged auntie.

"So you thought you'd go for the more traditional chocolate spread and cheese option," Poppy grimaced, taking the sandwich, which was wrapped in enough cling film to keep the entire contents of their fridge fresh.

"You can be very narrow-minded sometimes, Poppy. You really need to broaden your horizons."

She gave him a withering smile. "Thanks for the advice, little brother." Peeling back the sandwich, she sniffed it cautiously. "Gross," she grumbled, nibbling a corner. It was surprisingly tasty. Who knew?

"It's not as bad as it sounds," she conceded, taking a huge bite.

Charlie smirked. "Told you so."

After their picnic Poppy followed Charlie into the cottage. She left him poking around in the kitchen and headed up the rickety staircase. She was keen to see if Caitlyn had left anything else under the floorboards. Ducking her head, she entered the larger of the two bedrooms. She paused. Was it her imagination or did the room feel different somehow? She narrowed her eyes and tried to remember how it had looked on their last visit. The old hessian sack was still in the corner next to the broken floorboard Charlie had put his foot through. He had piled the two wooden crates on top of each other in front of the window. Poppy checked to see if the baby swallows were still in their nest in the eaves and smiled as she counted four orange beaks.

"Should have saved you some of Charlie's sandwiches," she told them.

She kneeled on the floor, carefully prised open the broken floorboard and peered inside. A black beetle scuttled away, its antennae waving furiously. As it disappeared under a joist Poppy noticed a glint of metal. She reached in and pulled out a silver trophy. The silver had tarnished in places, but it was easy enough to read the inscription. *South Devon Open Showjumping Competition. 1st place: Jodie Morgan and Nethercote Nero.*

Charlie was outside with Cloud by the time Poppy had hidden the trophy under the floorboards and gone back downstairs. She tightened Cloud's girth, ran down his stirrups and swung into the saddle. She stared at the grimy bedroom window. Something about the room was niggling her.

"Why did you move the crates?" she asked Charlie finally.

He looked at her in confusion. "I didn't. I thought you must have."

"How could I? I went up after you." Poppy gave an involuntary shiver. "If I didn't move them, and you didn't move them, who did?"

CHAPTER 8

Poppy and Charlie had emerged from the dark canopy of conifers when Charlie stopped pedalling and pointed straight ahead.

"Someone's coming."

Poppy halted Cloud and squinted into the sun. She could just about make out a chestnut-coloured blob in the distance. "It's only a Dartmoor pony."

"You need to get your eyes tested." Charlie reached in his pocket for his small birdwatching binoculars. "It's someone riding. Look."

He handed the binoculars to Poppy. Charlie was right. A horse and rider were cantering towards them. The horse had four white socks and a flaxen mane and tail.

"It's Red!" Poppy exclaimed.

"I thought you horsey people called it chestnut, like white is always grey?" said Charlie.

"No, you twit. It's Red. Scarlett's new horse. But what's he doing here?" She trained the binoculars on the slim girl riding the chestnut gelding. She would have recognised the determined set of her shoulders a mile off. "And Jodie," she said, handing the binoculars back to Charlie.

"Let's go and say hello."

"OK. But don't mention we've been to Witch Cottage," Poppy told him.

"Er, why would I? It's our secret place."

Red's flanks were dark with sweat as Jodie pulled him up a few metres from them.

"What are you two doing here?" she said warily.

"Just out for a hack," said Poppy. "We took a picnic," she said, pointing to the saddlebags.

Jodie's face cleared. "It's a lovely day for it. I decided to make time for one last ride before Red goes to Scarlett's in the morning."

"She's beyond excited. She's spent hours getting everything ready for him. He's going to be treated like royalty," Poppy told her.

Jodie ran her hand down the gelding's neck. "King Red. It suits him."

"Are you heading back? We could ride with you some of the way."

Red stretched his neck towards Cloud and gave a low whinny. The Connemara pricked his ears and whickered back. Jodie glanced briefly towards the belt of conifers and checked her watch.

"Sure. Why not? I've got to get back for evening stables anyway. It'll give the boys a chance to get to know each other."

Poppy smiled as Cloud and Red's noses touched. "I think they're going to get along just fine."

That evening, after checking her dad, Caroline and Charlie were safely downstairs engrossed in an episode of Dr Who, Poppy closed her bedroom door, reached in her sock drawer and pulled out Caitlyn's diary. She sat on her wicker chair with a cushion on her lap and turned to the last entry.

I am sitting on the banks of the tarn as I write this, dangling my feet in the icy water. Cloud keeps trying to nibble my pen. Nero is dozing next to him and Jodie is watching the swallows feeding their babies in the nest in the eaves.

So now I've set the scene.

I feel both happy and sad. Is that even possible? Happy because Jodie and I have had a brilliant summer, riding, competing and just hanging out here at 'our' cottage together with the ponies away from the Annoying Parents. Sad because it's the last day of the summer holidays and this time on Monday I won't be daydreaming here by the tarn, I'll be sitting in a stuffy classroom bored out of my mind. Riding will have to fit in around school and homework and when I can persuade Mum to give me a lift up to Gran's. It sucks. The only thing I've got to look forward to is the hunter trial at Widecombe. Jodie's not doing it - it's showjumping or nothing for her - but she's promised to come and be my groom for the day.

Back to today. Jodie and I wanted to mark the cottage as our territory. Tigers wee or scratch the bark of trees. Not us! We decided to each leave something of ours here, to lay claim to it. So I'm going to leave my diary and Jodie's going to leave the trophy she won at the South Devon show. We've found a loose floorboard in the big bedroom and we're going to hide them under it. I wonder if anyone will ever find them??

So I'm signing off now. I was getting too old for diaries

anyway. If I need to offload I tell Cloud. He's the official Keeper of my Secrets. LOVE that pony!! It's so long from me. See ya on the other side! :)

Poppy stared at the smiley face until her vision blurred with tears. Caitlyn had been so excited about the hunter trial at Widecombe. She'd had no idea that catastrophic disaster lay around the corner. All it took was a slippery drop fence and a moment's loss of concentration and her fate was sealed. What if Cloud hadn't been spooked by the crowds? What if she hadn't decided to compete? What if it hadn't rained?

Poppy knew that worrying about the what ifs got you precisely nowhere, but even so. Caitlyn would be the same age as Jodie now, and Cloud would still be hers, not Poppy's. She hid the diary back in her sock drawer and peered out of the window. Cloud and Chester were standing nose to tail by the gate, their tails swishing lazily. As if he had a sixth sense, Cloud lifted his head, saw her watching and whickered. Poppy brushed the tears from her cheeks. Did it matter that he'd been Caitlyn's first? For the first time in her life she realised she hadn't felt the usual dart of jealousy at the thought of Caitlyn and Cloud together. All she felt was intense sadness that Cait's future had been wrenched from her so cruelly.

Had Jodie acted as Caitlyn's groom that fateful day? Poppy pictured the brusque blonde girl standing with Tory and Cait's mum Jo on the sidelines, her hands full of grooming kit and bandages as she cheered horse and rider on as they'd galloped up to the drop fence, her eyes widening in horror as Cloud twisted in mid-air, lost his footing and somersaulted over, throwing Cait underneath him.

Poppy tried to imagine how she would feel if it was Scarlett tumbling to the muddy ground in a tangle of flailing limbs. It didn't bear thinking about. The image was so vivid she could almost hear the gasps of shock and the wail of sirens. She shivered. Poor Jodie. And poor Caitlyn.

Thoughts of the accident consumed Poppy's thoughts for the rest of the evening. It wasn't until she was lying in bed, staring at the ceiling, that she remembered the wooden crates. Caitlyn and Jodie may have marked the cottage as their territory. But someone else had now muscled in.

CHAPTER 9

"So, what d'you think?" Scarlett asked, chewing her bottom lip. "Is it good enough?"

Poppy surveyed the stable next to Blaze's. Up until a couple of days ago it had been used to store farm machinery and spare feed troughs. Every inch had been scrubbed and swept. Scarlett had laid a thick bed of straw and filled the hay rack with new hay. Two water-filled buckets stood in old rubber tyres. There was even a mineral lick attached to the ring by the door. Scarlett was hopping from one foot to the other. Poppy had never seen her look so nervous.

"It looks awesome!" she said. "You've done a brilliant job. Jodie's going to be super impressed and Red's going to love it."

"Are you sure?"

"'Course I'm sure. What time are they due?"

"Ten o'clock. What time is it now?"

Poppy checked her watch. "Quarter to."

Scarlett groaned. "Fifteen whole minutes! That's *ages*."

"Come on, let's groom Blaze and Flynn. It'll pass the time."

At ten past ten they heard the rattle of Jodie's Land Rover and trailer as it negotiated the potholed farm drive. Scarlett dropped the body brush and curry comb she'd been holding and clutched Blaze's neck in excitement.

"Oh my God, they're here! I must go and tell Mum."

Poppy smiled indulgently as her best friend sprinted towards the back door. Jodie parked the Land Rover and jumped out.

"All ready for King Red?" she asked.

Poppy grinned, curtseyed and gestured to the immaculate stable. "His palace awaits, ma'am. I'm surprised Scarlett didn't manage to find a roll of red carpet for his majesty."

Jodie glanced inside and raised her eyebrows. "I see what you mean. I think we can safely say Scarlett's passed the home visit. It puts Nethercote to shame. Red won't know he's born."

Scarlett appeared, followed closely by Pat, who was carrying a tray laden with mugs of tea and a chocolate cake.

"Hello Jodie love. I thought I'd bake a cake to celebrate Red's arrival," Pat said, setting the tray on the bonnet of the Land Rover. Jodie pulled down the ramp of the trailer, unloaded Red and handed Scarlett his leadrope.

The chestnut gelding's head was high and his nostrils flared as he took in his new surroundings.

"Red, I'd like to introduce you to Flynn," said Scarlett. Flynn turned his head briefly and returned to his haynet, unimpressed by the new arrival. "And this is Blaze." Blaze and Red blew into each other's nostrils, their ears pricked. Blaze squealed loudly, throwing one hoof in the air. "Be nice!" Scarlett scolded her.

"It's probably a good idea not to turn them out together for a couple of days. Let them get used to each other," said Jodie.

She and Scarlett settled Red into his pristine stable while Pat cut generous slices of cake.

Jodie poked her head over the stable door. "Poppy, can you get the adoption certificate? It's on the passenger seat."

Poppy heaved open the heavy door of the Land Rover. The seat was covered in sweet wrappers, loops of baler twine, empty wormer packets and unopened envelopes that looked suspiciously like bills. She rummaged through the detritus, finding what she was looking for at the bottom. As she tugged on the sheet of white card bearing the Nethercote logo and the words *Certificate of Adoption* she dislodged Jodie's iPhone and it slid into a gap between the seat and the gearstick.

Sighing, Poppy stretched her arm into the gap and grabbed the phone. It beeped. She dropped it in surprise and it slithered right under the seat.

"Damn," she muttered, tucking her hair behind her ears and feeling for the phone again. This time she pulled it out and without thinking scanned the text on the home screen.

Delivery tonight. Leave cash as agreed. Used notes or deal's off. You have been warned.

A voice behind Poppy made her start.

"Did you find it?"

Poppy shoved the phone back under the envelopes and sweet wrappers and smiled brightly at Jodie.

"Here it is!"

"Great. Let's celebrate with a slice of cake and then I must be off. There's somewhere I need to be."

Charlie was smacking a golf ball around the garden with one of their dad's old five irons when Poppy arrived home.

"Guess what?" he said, his tongue between his teeth as he flexed his knees and lined up for a shot.

"Tiger Woods has asked you to take his place in next year's Open Championship?"

"Ha ha, very funny." Charlie lifted the club and swung at the ball. Shielding his eyes, he scanned the sky. "Where did it go?" he asked, puzzled.

"It's still there." Poppy pointed at his feet.

He stared at the pitted white ball nestling in the grass. "Oh." He took another swipe. They both watched as the ball sailed in a graceful arc, smashing the glass on one of Caroline's cold frames. Charlie's face paled.

"You are going to be in *so* much trouble," Poppy told him.

He thought for a moment, worry lines creasing his forehead. Then his face cleared. "I know! I'll mend it with Dad's Super Glue."

"I'm not sure that's going to work. Anyway, what were you going to tell me?"

Charlie pointed the club at the sky.

Poppy sighed. "What exactly am I supposed to be looking at?"

"The moon," said Charlie. "The *full* moon," he added dramatically.

Poppy looked again. There, peeping behind a cloud almost apologetically, as if it had turned up to a party uninvited, was the muted, perfectly spherical face of the moon.

"And?" said Poppy, bemused.

Charlie looked left and right to check no-one was in earshot, then whispered furtively, "We can go to Witch Cottage and see if the legend is true."

"What, Scarlett's supernatural claptrap about the old crone and Marmalade and the burning cloak?" Poppy scoffed. "Of course it's not true!"

"It's Marmaduke actually, and how can you be so sure?"

"Because there are no such things as ghosts or witches, Charlie. It's an old wives' tale, I promise you."

Charlie nodded to himself. "I might have known."

"Might have known what?" she said sharply.

"That you'd claim it was rubbish because really you were too frightened to go."

Poppy bristled. "I am not! Alright then, if it means that much to you we'll go. We'll wait until Dad and Caroline are asleep and ride Cloud over together. Happy now?"

Charlie whooped and sprinted towards the house, the golf club and shattered cold frame forgotten. As she watched him go, Poppy had the distinct impression she had been played like the proverbial fiddle by a master manipulator.

CHAPTER 10

The sky was a deep indigo as Poppy and Charlie crept out of the house and headed for the stables. After waiting so patiently the moon had taken centre stage and was glowing with pearlescent luminosity, encircled by a smattering of glittering stars.

Cloud was dozing at the back of the stable he shared with Chester, but lifted his head and whickered when he heard the bolt slide open. Poppy offered them a handful of pony nuts, slipped on Cloud's bridle and led him into the yard. Charlie handed Poppy her riding hat and fastened up the straps of his cycling helmet.

"You'll be fine as long as you hold on tight," she whispered, leading Cloud over to the low stone wall she used as a mounting block. "I'll get on first."

Once she was satisfied Charlie was safely on and his arms were wrapped around her waist, she clicked her tongue and turned Cloud towards the moor.

The Connemara was as excited as Charlie about their night-time adventure and jogged up the track towards the Riverdale tor. Poppy could feel her brother's warm breath on the back of her neck as she eased her pony back into a walk.

"You OK?" she asked.

"You bet!" he cried. "This is awesome!"

Charlie had brought his digital camera, convinced he was going to snap a shot of the old witch as she glided around the banks of the tarn. Poppy had slipped her mobile in her back pocket, just in case. Adventures with her brother often ended up with a trip to accident and emergency. She wanted to be prepared.

Cloud's mane was burnished silver in the moonlight and his neck was arched. All he needed were wings and he could be Pegasus.

"Do you think you'll be alright to go a bit faster, if we take it steady?" Poppy called.

"Uh huh," Charlie said, tightening his grip.

Poppy squeezed her legs and Cloud broke into a canter. He was as surefooted as the black-faced sheep that every so often loomed out of the darkness, the glow of their eyes just visible in the inky light. It was exhilarating, racing across the wide, open moor in the dead of night, and a smile crept across Poppy's face. Charlie clung on like a limpet.

"I thought riding was for girls and sissies but this is brilliant! When we get home can you teach me?"

"'Course I can. We'll ask Scarlett to lend us Flynn."

Ahead Poppy could just make out the shadowy strip of conifers that hid Witch Cottage from view. "Nearly there," she whispered.

Cloud slowed to a walk. The squelch of his hooves as he crossed the peaty ground sounded unnaturally loud in the still night air. He plunged into the darkness of the trees without hesitation. The conifers towered over them, their branches like twisted limbs, and Poppy felt her pulse quicken. She checked the luminous hands of her watch. Five to midnight. Ghosts or no ghosts, this was seriously spooky.

Cloud shifted and swerved through the trees. Eventually they reached the edge of the narrow forest. Poppy asked the Connemara to halt and he stood quietly as she peered into the gloom. The silhouette of Witch Cottage was as elusive and unformed as the first strokes of a watercolour painting.

"Now what?" she whispered.

"We should stay hidden in the trees, just in case," said Charlie, slithering to the ground.

"In case of what?" Poppy jumped off, too, and held Cloud's reins tightly.

"Old crones and ginger cats, of course." Charlie's grinning teeth gleamed in the moonlight.

They stood in silence either side of Cloud. Charlie fiddled with his camera. Poppy scuffed the ground with the toe of her jodhpur boot. She felt as conspicuous as an angel perched atop a Christmas tree, and not a little foolish. She stifled a yawn. Why on earth had she agreed to let Charlie drag her into the middle of nowhere in the middle of the night on such a crazy adventure?

After ten minutes in the dank shadows Poppy was starting to feel the cold. She turned to her brother. "Come on, Charlie. Let's go home. There's patently no-one here. Not even a ghost is silly enough to be out at this time of night."

"Five more minutes?" he pleaded.

Poppy hugged herself and exhaled loudly. "Alright

then. But I am never, ever coming on one of your stupid adventures again. Got it?"

"Thanks, sis." Charlie ducked under Cloud's neck. Soon he was twiddling with his camera again, pointing it at the cottage and zooming the lens in and out.

Poppy was stifling another yawn when he clutched her arm and whispered urgently, "There's a light in the cottage."

"Absolutely Hilarious with a capital H," Poppy whispered back, rolling her eyes.

"No, really Poppy, there is. Look!"

The tremor in his voice made Poppy grab the camera. She pointed it at the cottage. At first she thought the glow in the upstairs bedroom was moonlight reflecting off the window.

"Is it the old crone's burning cloak?" stammered Charlie. "I knew Scarlett was telling the truth."

Poppy shook her head. The beam of light was moving, as if a powerful torch was being waved around. Cloud had stiffened, his head high as he stared intently ahead. Charlie gripped her arm even tighter.

"Look at that!"

Poppy followed his gaze and gasped. A pick-up truck was rolling silently down the hill towards the cottage. They watched, transfixed, as two burly-looking men let themselves out, pulled an old tarpaulin off the back of the beaten-up truck and started unloading wooden crates.

"What are they *doing*?" breathed Charlie.

Poppy held her finger to her lips. The men were talking to each other in low voices, pointing to the light in the window. One took a mobile out of his pocket and started tapping furiously. The other picked up a crate, ducked under the low door frame and disappeared into the cottage.

Cloud shifted uneasily. Poppy rubbed his forehead and willed him to stay quiet. The man with the phone hefted a crate onto his hip. Once he was inside the cottage Poppy turned to her brother. "I don't like this. We should go."

"But -"

"No buts, Charlie. I don't know what those men are up to, but I don't think we should hang around to find out. They don't look the type to be messed with."

Not giving him the chance to argue, she led Cloud over to a fallen tree and vaulted on, holding her hand out for Charlie to follow suit. He clambered on, looking wistfully over his shoulder as she turned Cloud for home.

Once clear of the conifers Poppy pushed Cloud into a canter, keen to put as much distance as she could between them and the two shadowy men.

CHAPTER 11

"You look washed out. Are you feeling OK?" Caroline looked at Poppy in concern as she nibbled on a piece of toast the next morning.

"I'm fine." Poppy smiled briefly at her stepmother and took a slurp of orange juice. The truth was she was shattered. After they'd slunk back into the house she'd been so wired sleep had been impossible. She'd lain in bed, her imagination working overtime as she'd wondered about the men at Witch Cottage and, more importantly, the crates they'd been carrying.

A text from Scarlett was a welcome distraction.

Are we riding this morning or what??!! I have a new pony to try out you know!!

Poppy took a final swig of juice and tapped a message back.

'Course we're riding :) I'll be over in 20 mins x

Red's chestnut coat shone and his four socks were dazzlingly white. Scarlett had even pulled his mane and oiled his hooves.

"Blimey, you must have been up at the crack of dawn," said Poppy. Cloud, who had grass stains on his hocks and a tangled mane and tail, looked positively scruffy in comparison.

"I woke up at four I was so excited," Scarlett said. "I've been getting him ready since six. He's even had a bath. With warm water, of course."

"Of course," said Poppy. Scarlett used the hose on Blaze and Flynn.

"Where shall we go?" said Scarlett.

"I want to head over towards Witch Cottage."

"Not *again*. You and Charlie are obsessed with that place."

"Ah, but wait until you hear this." Poppy told her best friend about their nocturnal visit and the men they'd seen. Scarlett's jaw hit the floor.

"I can't believe I missed it. I wish you'd told me you were going."

"You won't even go near the place in the middle of the day. Would you have really wanted to come on Charlie's ghost hunt at midnight?"

"Probably not," Scarlett admitted. "Do you think you should call the police?"

"What would I tell them? It was too dark to get proper descriptions or see their number plate. I don't even know if they were doing anything illegal. That's why I want to see what's in those crates they delivered."

"I'd forgotten how close it is to the prison," said Poppy, gazing at the granite walls of HMP Dartmoor, the two ponies walking side-by-side.

"We went to the museum there last summer," said Scarlett.

Poppy raised her eyebrows. "There's a museum at the prison?"

Scarlett nodded. "You should go. Charlie would love it. They've got all the weapons the warders used to use on the prisoners, like straitjackets, manacles and cat o'nine tails, and the knuckledusters and other weapons the convicts made. It's really interesting."

Poppy pictured the two thickset men she and Charlie had seen the night before and her heart missed a beat. "Do prisoners still escape?"

"They used to, in the olden days," said Scarlett. "It's only a Category C prison now. The prisoners are low risk. They make gnomes and toadstools to sell as garden ornaments, can you believe? Mum bought one for her rose garden."

Poppy couldn't imagine the two men they'd seen the night before painting red hats and impish grins onto stone gnomes. The fact that Witch Cottage was so close to the prison was a coincidence, she told herself.

Scarlett elected to hold the ponies while Poppy scooted across to the dilapidated stone building. The minute she walked through the door it felt different. The air, which had smelt so fusty the first time she'd explored the cottage, was alive with static. She ran lightly up the stairs to the first bedroom, expecting to find it piled high with crates. But the room was empty apart from the two wooden boxes still stacked by the window. Were they the same as the ones the men had unloaded from the pick-up? Poppy inspected the room, her eyes narrowed, searching for any clue. There were marks on the floor. Had they been there before? And had the doorframe always been cracked? She couldn't remember.

Frustrated, she walked around the room a second

time, examining every inch. Her attention was caught by the hum of a mosquito. She watched it as it spiralled up towards the ceiling and landed on the loft hatch.

"Poppy!" Everything OK?"

Poppy yanked open the ancient window and stuck her head out. Scarlett was sitting on the old stone wall with Cloud and Red grazing next to her.

"Just coming," Poppy shouted back.

Halfway down the stairs she stopped, shook her head at her own foolishness, and sprinted back up. The ceiling was so low in the tiny bedroom that she could almost touch it if she stood on her toes. She pulled one of the boxes into the centre of the room, climbed onto it and gave the loft hatch a tentative shove. It lifted easily. Poppy poked her head into the roof space. Expecting darkness she was surprised to see a patch of blue sky in the corner, then remembered the hole in the catslide roof.

She jumped off the box, carried the second one over and stacked them on top of each other. Now the ceiling was level with her shoulders and Poppy was sure she would be able to climb in. Testing her weight on the frame of the hatch, she looked around, taking in the shafts of sunlight, the swirling particles of decades-old dust, long-abandoned swallows' nests and the smell of dead mouse.

In the middle of the attic was the brick chimney breast. Behind it flapped the corner of a green tarpaulin. Her heart hammering, Poppy hauled herself through the hatch. A rusty nail caught her shin and she yelped in pain. The roof of the attic was so low she had to bend double. She crabbed sideways along one of the worm-ridden beams and peered around the chimney breast.

Hidden under the green tarpaulin were around a dozen wooden crates. Poppy pulled the closest one towards her and prised open the lid.

"Mobile phones?" said Scarlett, her face perplexed.

Poppy nodded. "Dozens of smartphones of all different makes. They were still in their boxes with the Cellophane on and everything."

"And nothing else?"

"Nope."

Scarlett looked around her fearfully, as if she was being watched. "I knew this place was cursed. It was a mistake to come back." She swung into the saddle and turned Red for home.

The chestnut gelding disappeared into the trees and Poppy had to trot to catch up. "What are they doing there, that's what I want to know."

"I don't know and I don't care. We should let the police deal with it, Poppy. Go and see that inspector you saw before."

Poppy thought of the wide-girthed Inspector Bill Pearson and his penchant for digestive biscuits. Perhaps she should phone the police but a niggling voice in the back of her head told her she'd be wasting their time. "Maybe."

Seeing the worry on Scarlett's face she changed the subject. "How's Red? Are you pleased with your new pony?"

"Pleased?" Scarlett reached down and patted the chestnut gelding's neck. "I am beyond happy. He is the most gorgeous, lovely, brilliant horse in the world."

"Apart from Cloud," Poppy corrected her.

Scarlett laughed, the mobile phones pushed to the back of her mind, and she spent the rest of the ride home extolling Red's countless virtues. Poppy smiled and agreed in all the right places, but her thoughts were in a tiny attic under a catslide roof, where dust motes danced and faceless men stashed their ill-gotten gains under slippery green tarpaulins.

CHAPTER 12

At breakfast the following morning Caroline announced a shopping trip to Plymouth. Poppy's shoulders slumped.

"Torture," muttered Charlie into his Shreddies.

"You've grown so much this summer your trousers could pass as shorts. We'll have to either stop feeding you or start balancing books on your head," Caroline told him. "Poppy, you need a new blazer and school skirt. And you both need new school shoes. It's not long until the start of term."

"Don't remind us," grumbled Poppy. Although she couldn't say she actually hated school, she had so many more interesting things she could be doing than learning about poems and probability. And the prospect of standing in a manically busy shoe shop holding a ticket in her hand waiting to have her feet measured on a sweaty measuring machine while dozens of out-of-control toddlers weaved around her legs did not appeal.

"We'll pop into Baxters' on the way home if you

like?"

Slightly mollified, Poppy nodded. She never passed up an opportunity to spend half an hour looking around the leather-scented tack and feed store on the Tavistock road.

Their shopping expedition was as torturous as Charlie had predicted, the only highlight being a bowl of pasta in a little Italian restaurant on the Barbican. Poppy drooled over the black leather jumping saddles and matching bridles in Baxters' and treated Cloud and Chester to a new leadrope each. On their way home Caroline remembered they needed eggs and pulled in outside Waterby Post Office and Stores.

"Hey, isn't that Scarlett?" Charlie said.

Through the glass window, which was pebble-dashed with posters advertising choral events, coffee mornings and rams for sale, Poppy saw her best friend ringing up someone's shopping on the till, watched by the twinkly-eyed shopkeeper Barney Broomfield. "I'd forgotten it was her first shift at the shop this afternoon."

Poppy waited until Scarlett had rung up an elderly lady's copy of the Radio Times and a tin of pitted prunes and asked, "How's it going?"

"OK, I think," said Scarlett, looking slightly flustered. "Barney says it'll be brilliant for my mental arithmetic but I'm not so sure." She sniffed her fingers and pulled a face. "And my hands smell of money."

Charlie jiggled coins in his shorts pocket. "Can I have forty five pence worth of rhubarb and custards, please Scarlett."

"Sure." As Scarlett lifted the jar of sweets from a shelf she mouthed to Poppy, "Look at the front page of the Herald!"

There was a pile of Tavistock Heralds by the front door. Poppy sidled over. The headline was like a punch in the solar plexus.

Exclusive: Police launch investigation after daring theft of mobile phones
By Stanley Smith

Blood pounding in her ears, Poppy picked up the top copy and scanned the article.

Police have launched an investigation after mobile phones worth £20,000 were stolen during a daring raid on a Plymouth warehouse.
The thieves disabled CCTV cameras and locked the security guard in his office before helping themselves to dozens of top-of-the-range Apple, Samsung and Sony smartphones.
"The phones were taken overnight on 15 August, and we are appealing for anyone who has information about the burglary to contact us," said a police spokesman.

"Do you want to know a secret?" whispered a voice in her ear. Poppy jumped like a scalded cat, but it was only Charlie, brandishing a small paper bag of rhubarb and custards. "Scarlett gave me an extra one for luck! You can have it if you like."

Poppy changed into jodhpurs and a tee-shirt the minute they arrived home. Hoping a ride on the moor might clear her head, she caught Cloud, gave him a cursory groom and tacked him up. Soon they were cantering towards the Riverdale tor. At the top Poppy slid to the ground, sat cross-legged on a flat granite boulder and shared an apple with her pony as she gazed at the sweeping panorama. Directly ahead, sandwiched between their two paddocks, was the slate roof of Riverdale. Poppy could just make out a Chester-shaped brown blob by the water trough. The McKeevers' gravel drive ran parallel to the track to Ashworthy. Scarlett's home was an archetypical working farm. An old, slightly shabby farmhouse surrounded by a jumble of barns, stables and outhouses. Scarlett loved houses with clean modern lines, all glass and steel, but Poppy adored Ashworthy's low ceilings and mullioned windows.

She couldn't see Witch Cottage from here. Even the chimneys of Dartmoor Prison were hidden behind a distant tor.

"What should I do, Cloud?"

The Connemara rubbed his head on her tee-shirt, leaving a layer of short, white hairs on the navy brushed cotton.

"Tell the police, tell Dad and Caroline, or try to find out who stole the mobiles myself?"

Telling the police or her parents was the obvious, sensible thing to do, Poppy knew that. But that would mean admitting she had lied *and* that she had dragged Charlie to a crime scene in the middle of the night. She had a feeling they wouldn't be impressed.

"I wonder what Caitlyn would have done if she were me," she pondered. Cloud pricked his ears at the sound of Cait's name, as he always did. But Poppy no longer felt resentful. She wished Cait was still alive. She felt sure they'd have been friends if things had been different.

Cait wasn't around to ask, but Jodie was. Jodie knew Witch Cottage. She was both smart and tough. Poppy had a feeling Jodie wouldn't judge her for not phoning the police. She made up her mind.

Tomorrow she would cycle over to Nethercote.

Jodie would know what to do.

CHAPTER 13

Nethercote's tall chimneys cast shadows at her feet as Poppy pushed her bike up the drive. It was late afternoon and the sun burned orange in the sky. She'd told Caroline she was cycling to Scarlett's, but instead she'd turned in the opposite direction and had followed the narrow lanes to the horse rescue sanctuary.

Poppy walked past the ivy-clad farmhouse to the stables. The yard was quiet save for the reassuringly familiar sound of horses chomping their suppers, and they lifted their heads to watch her from their stable doors as she passed.

There was no sign of Jodie.

Poppy rang the bell outside the feed room but it failed to summon the older girl. Poppy dithered, not wanting to knock on the door of the house. She sidled over to Biscuit's stable and stroked the appaloosa's spotted face.

"Where's Jodie?" she asked the rescue pony. "I need to talk to her."

"I'm here."

Poppy spun around. Jodie was behind her, a water bucket in each hand.

"What did you want to talk to me about?"

Poppy didn't know where to start. "It's a long story. Is there somewhere we can sit down?"

"Sure. Follow me." Jodie set the buckets down, splashing water over her boots. She led Poppy through the feed room to a tack room beyond. One wall was lined with saddle racks. Bridles hung from hooks on another. The only light came from a tiny, grimy window on the back wall. The old stone walls had leached any warmth from the room. Poppy shivered.

Jodie flicked a switch. A strip light flickered and died. "Bloody light. Yet another thing that needs fixing." She waved Poppy to a shabby tub chair in front of an ancient electric fire. "What's up? It's not Red, is it?"

"Red's fine. He seems to have settled in and Scarlett's still treating him like royalty. We hacked out yesterday and he was as good as gold. Nothing to worry about there." Poppy realised she was gabbling.

Jodie raised her eyebrows. "So what's the problem?"

"You and Caitlyn were best friends, weren't you?"

Jodie fiddled with a loose strand of cotton on the arm of her chair. Her fingers were trembling. "Did Tory tell you?"

"I haven't seen Tory for ages. I found an old newspaper clipping. You competed in the South Devon Open Showjumping Competition together. You won it."

"And Caitlyn was second. Boy was she sore about that."

"Why didn't you say anything when you recognised Cloud at the fete?"

"Seeing him brought it all back. I've spent the last seven years trying to forget what happened," said Jodie.

"I'm sorry."

"Why should you be? It wasn't your fault. It wasn't anyone's fault. It was one of those things. He's a lovely pony. I'm glad he's found a good home."

"Do you still have Nero?" Poppy asked.

Jodie's features darkened. "He went when Dad went...*away*. If that's it I'd better get on. There are a hundred and one things I should be doing."

"There was something else," Poppy said. "It's about Witch Cottage."

Jodie was still for a second, then shrugged. "Never heard of it."

"The old cottage on the moor towards Princetown that's supposed to be haunted. Where the wild swimmer drowned."

Jodie shook her head. "Sorry, I don't know what you're talking about."

"But you do!" Poppy cried. "I know you and Cait used to hang out there. I found her diary and your trophy under the floorboards. Exactly where you'd left them." Poppy took Jodie's silence as an invitation to continue. "I've found something else in the cottage. Something that shouldn't be there. And I don't know what to do."

"What have you found?" Jodie asked sharply.

The palms of Poppy's hands felt sticky. She wiped them on her jodhpurs. "Mobile phones. Dozens of them. All brand new. They're hidden under a tarpaulin in the attic."

"What's that got to do with me?"

"I don't know what to do about them," said Poppy.

"Have you told anyone else?"

"Only Scarlett. She says I should call the police."

Jodie wound the cotton around her index finger and gave it a sharp tug. The thread snapped. She met Poppy's eyes. "And will you?"

"Will I what?"

"Call the police?"

"I don't know. That's why I wanted to talk to you."

"I'm all ears," said Jodie, flicking the cotton onto the floor.

"I think the phones are the ones that were stolen from the warehouse in Plymouth. There was a story about it in this week's Herald."

Jodie stared at the tackroom's pitted ceiling. "So what if they were? I still don't get what this has got to do with me."

"You know what I'm talking about," said Poppy.

Jodie stiffened. "What did you say?"

"I don't mean you know about the phones. You know about the cottage. I wanted to talk it through with someone who understood."

Jodie exhaled slowly. "I understand alright."

"So you'll help?" Poppy felt giddy with relief.

Jodie jumped to her feet and grabbed the Land Rover keys from a hook by the door. Her mouth had tightened into a hard, thin line. "I think you'd better show me."

Jodie was silent as the Land Rover bumped along the stony track towards the cottage. Poppy stared out of the window. There were a hundred questions she wanted to ask. Top of the list was why Jodie was claiming to have never heard of the cottage when she and Cait had practically spent their last summer together there. But one glance at Jodie's granite-like profile was enough to make her bite her tongue.

They rounded a bend and the cottage came into view. From this distance you couldn't see the hole in the roof and the rotting windows. Poppy imagined smoke curling from the chimney and a white-haired man with stooped shoulders tending a vegetable patch, watched by an elderly border collie.

Jodie pulled in alongside the tarn, braking so sharply that Poppy's seatbelt bit into her shoulder. The older girl sat for a while, her hands clutching the steering wheel. Somewhere in the Land Rover a mobile phone pinged with a new text message, but Jodie continued staring blankly ahead. Poppy found her stillness unnerving. Surreptitiously she felt her back pocket for her own mobile. It wasn't there. She'd meant to pick it up from the worktop in the kitchen where she'd left it charging but had been in such a hurry to leave that she'd clean forgotten.

When Jodie turned to face Poppy, her face was expressionless. "Let's go."

"The mobiles are in the attic. I can show you, if you like. There are a couple of wooden boxes you can stand on so you're high enough to see. There's a hole in the roof but there's a tarpaulin over them to keep them dry. Whoever hid them here planned it properly," Poppy said, climbing the stairs. She knew she was babbling again but she couldn't help herself.

"Oh, it was planned alright," Jodie said, following Poppy into the biggest bedroom. She pointed to the two boxes. "Sit down."

"Don't you want me to show you where they are?"

85

Jodie shook her head. "Sit down," she repeated.

Poppy did as she was told. Jodie walked to the window. She glanced over her shoulder at Poppy. "I already know where they are."

"I don't understand."

"I know where they are because I put them there."

CHAPTER 14

Poppy gaped at Jodie. Sunlight streamed through the window but the older girl's profile was in shadow.

"What do you mean, you put them there?"

"I told you my dad deals in mobile phones."

Poppy cast her mind back to the day they'd first visited Nethercote and Jodie had mentioned her dad ran an import business. But this was all wrong. Questions bubbled up inside her.

"But why is he storing them in a tumbledown cottage in the middle of nowhere? Is it because they were stolen from the warehouse in Plymouth? Where exactly *is* your dad, Jodie?"

"He's precisely two and a half miles north of here, staying full board at Her Majesty's pleasure."

"What do you mean?"

Jodie gave an impatient shake of her head, as if she couldn't believe Poppy's naivety.

"He's in the slammer. The clink. He's a guest of HMP Dartmoor. He's in *prison*, Poppy. My dad the convict is serving time."

Poppy swallowed. "What did he do?"

"He didn't kill anyone or anything like that. He fiddled the books at the building company he worked for."

"Fiddled the books? What do you mean?"

"It's easy for finance directors to steal a little bit here and there without anyone noticing, apparently. Only he got greedy. And careless. The other directors were suspicious and called in the police. Dad was convicted five years ago."

"When you were still at school?"

Jodie laughed hollowly. "He was sent to prison a week before my GCSEs. I bombed the lot."

"I'm sorry."

"You keep apologising, don't you Poppy? Even when it's not your fault. You need to toughen up, kid. Else people will trample all over you."

Poppy recoiled at the bitterness in Jodie's voice. "I'm... I mean, why did he do it?"

"He set up the sanctuary with the money my grandparents left him when they died, figuring that he'd be able to raise enough money to pay for the running costs. Of course he couldn't. Any idiot could have told him that. But then Dad's a dreamer, always has been."

"So he used the money he'd stolen to pay for the horses?" Poppy said.

Jodie nodded. "He wanted me to follow my dream, too, so he bought Nero and a top-of-the range horsebox so we could compete all over the South West. Mum turned a blind eye to his thieving and I never knew until the morning the police turned up at the house and arrested him."

"What happened to Nero?"

"The police took everything of value because they said it was proceeds of crime, including Nero. I'll never forgive Dad for that."

"So you had to give it all up?"

"He left me with twenty four rescue horses to look after. I couldn't ride professionally any more."

"But you've managed to keep Nethercote going while he's been in prison," Poppy said.

"Only just. And now the money's all gone." Jodie stared out of the window. The silence in the tiny attic bedroom was stifling. Suddenly everything fell into place. The mysterious text message on Jodie's phone. Her dad's import business. The hidden mobiles. The towering granite walls of Dartmoor prison just a couple of miles away.

"You're going to try to smuggle those phones into the prison," Poppy whispered.

Jodie balled her hands into fists and Poppy felt her stomach clench. But the older girl didn't move.

"It was his idea. He can sell a mobile phone for a flippin' fortune inside."

"But how are you planning to -"

"Get them in? The wing Dad's in is nearest the perimeter wall. Two cells have windows looking out onto the moor. One on the fourth floor and the other directly above it. Dad's cell."

Jodie left the window and sat on the box next to Poppy.

"The prison's a listed building so his window hasn't got a grating over it. He's spent the last couple of days making a rope from bedding and is going to lower it out of the window and over the wall. I'll be at the bottom, waiting." She smiled mirthlessly. "I'll tie the bag of phones to his rope and he'll haul them up.

We'll make enough money in one night to keep the horses fed for a year."

"Did you steal the phones from the warehouse?" Poppy asked.

Jodie bristled. "I am not a thief. Not like *him*. He organised it all. I just met the men when they delivered the phones and hid them in the attic."

Without thinking Poppy said, "We didn't see you."

Jodie looked at her in astonishment. "*What?*"

Poppy glanced out of the window towards the conifers. "Charlie and I were watching from the trees."

"What the hell were you doing here?"

Poppy rubbed her hand across her forehead. It was all too much to take in. "Charlie wanted to see if the place was really haunted. We rode over on Cloud," she muttered.

"What if they'd seen you? Those men aren't the kind of people to mess with," Jodie said roughly.

Poppy had been through a whole gamut of emotions in the last half an hour. Shock. Anxiety. Fear. Incredulity. Suddenly anger superseded it all. "What if *we'd* been seen? What about you? If you get caught you'll go to jail! Who'll look after the rescue horses then?" she cried.

"Don't you understand? I have to do this. I have no choice."

Poppy shook her head in disbelief. "So why've you told me all this?"

Jodie stood up and stalked over to the window again. "I couldn't tell you at home because if my mum even gets a whiff that someone is onto us she'll go straight to the prison governor and incriminate Dad. She's already terrified I'll get caught. I couldn't risk you going to the police and reporting the phones. I had to stop you."

"Of course I've got to tell the police! Have you gone crazy?"

Jodie feigned surprise. "Well, well. Mild-mannered, quiet little Poppy actually has a backbone. Who'd have thought it?"

It was Poppy's turn to bristle. "I'm phoning them as soon as I get home."

Jodie's lips thinned again. "You can't. I'll be sent to jail and you're right, there is no-one else to look after the horses. They'll have to be put down and it'll be your fault. Percy, Mr Darcy. Even Biscuit. Can you live with that on your conscience?"

Jodie was bluffing, Poppy was sure of it. "Nethercote isn't the only horse rescue centre in Devon. There are dozens of them! Someone else will take them in."

"Are you willing to risk it? Anyway, you're implicated now. You lifted the tarpaulin to have a look at the phones, right?"

Poppy nodded, unsure where this was heading.

"Your prints will be all over it. All over the cottage, in fact. I'll tell the police I recruited you and your brother to act as scouts."

Poppy felt the blood drain from her face. "You wouldn't!"

"Needs must," Jodie said grimly. "It'll be your word against mine. And let me warn you, I'm a very good liar. I'll take you down with me, for the sake of the horses. For the sake of Nethercote."

CHAPTER 15

Poppy slumped onto the box again, her head in her hands. What if Jodie was telling the truth, that she really was prepared to incriminate her? She couldn't believe the police would actually think she'd been involved, but you read about miscarriages of justice in the papers all the time. And if they heard that the son and daughter of a BBC war correspondent had been questioned about a prison smuggling ring the tabloids would have a field day. Her dad would probably lose his job and they'd have to move. Suddenly she was struck by a thought so terrible it pierced her heart. Without Riverdale she'd have to sell Cloud and Chester. That's if she wasn't already doing time in a Young Offender's Institute.

"It's not nice, being forced into something you don't want to do because you have no choice, is it?" said Jodie. "Now you know how I feel. I don't want to break the law, but Dad gave me no alternative."

"When are you doing it?" Poppy asked dully.

"Tonight at eleven. The sooner the better as far as

I'm concerned."

"He'll make you do it again, you know that, don't you?"

For the first time Poppy saw a flicker of doubt cross Jodie's face. The older girl shook her head.

"I've told him it's a one-off."

"And you believe him, do you?"

Jodie gave an imperceptible nod.

"He probably even believes it himself," Poppy said. "When he decided to steal money from his company he probably told himself it would be the first and last time. But people get greedy. You said it yourself."

Jodie exhaled loudly and stalked out of the room. "It's happening tonight. End of."

They drove back to Nethercote in silence. As Jodie pulled into the drive Poppy made a last ditch attempt to change her mind.

"There must be other ways to raise the money. Scarlett and I will help you."

Jodie gave a short bark of laughter. "Two gormless thirteen-year-olds? I don't think so. It costs thousands of pounds a year to run this place. Where are you going to find that kind of money? In your piggy banks? Down the back of the sofa? I promise you, this is the only way."

"At least let us try."

Jodie grabbed her arm. "Haven't you been listening to anything I've said?" Her voice was thick with menace. Or was it unshed tears? Poppy couldn't be sure.

A door slammed. "There you are! I made bacon butties for tea but you'd disappeared," said Jodie's mum, appearing from the house.

Jodie let go of Poppy's arm, leaving a red hand-shaped imprint.

"I had a call about a mare that had been left tethered to a tree on the Tavistock road without food or water. Poppy and I drove over to have a look but we couldn't find her, could we, Poppy?"

Shocked at how smoothly Jodie had lied, Poppy said nothing.

Jodie's mum seemed oblivious to the undercurrents and smiled brightly. "Would you like a bacon butty, love? There's plenty to go around."

Poppy shook her head. "No thanks. I've lost my appetite. Anyway, I need to get going. My stepmum will be wondering where I am."

Poppy retrieved her bike but as she was about to pedal off, Jodie blocked her way.

"I'm not doing this for me or my dad. I'm doing it for the horses. So please, *please* don't tell anyone. You'll ruin everything."

Poppy rushed past, too appalled to reply. Unshed tears burned her throat and anxiety knotted her stomach. Jodie went to grab her handlebar but Poppy swerved out of the way. The bike almost lost traction on the gravel but Poppy stamped on the pedals and brought it back under control. Once on the main road she put her head down and cycled as fast as she could towards Riverdale, relishing the burning pain in her thigh muscles as she attacked each hill because it took her mind off everything else. She wished she could turn back the clock. She wished she'd never asked Jodie for advice, never found the mobile phones, never let Charlie talk her into going looking for his stupid ghosts. She longed for blissful ignorance. But deep in her heart she knew it was too late for that.

The question was, what could she do to make things right?

Poppy flung her bike on the grass and vaulted the gate to Cloud and Chester's paddock. The Connemara was dozing by the far hedge but opened his eyes and whickered with pleasure when Poppy called him. She threw her arms around him, breathing in lungfuls of his pure, horsey smell, imagining how awful it would be if they had to sell up and move away. She felt a sob rising in her throat at the thought of him being driven away in someone else's horsebox to a yard who knew where. The prospect was too terrible to bear and she collapsed onto the ground, tears streaming down her cheeks. When Cloud nuzzled her neck and blew softly into her ear she wailed even harder. She stayed like that, hugging her knees, with Cloud watching over her, until she was all cried out.

It was Chester who dragged her from her misery. The old donkey wandered over and gave her a determined nudge. As she gazed into his chocolate brown eyes she felt her resolve strengthen.

"I know, I'm being wet and pathetic," she said in a quavering voice. "What would Tory say? That every problem has a solution, that's what."

She wiped her nose on the bottom of her tee-shirt and climbed stiffly to her feet. "I just need to work out what it is."

Her dad was in the lounge watching cricket, with Magpie on his lap looking daggers at Freddie, who was lying at his feet, his raspberry-pink tongue lolling.

"Hello, daughter of mine." Mike McKeever patted the seat beside him.

Poppy sat down and tickled Magpie's chin. The cat

gave Freddie a supercilious look and began purring
loudly.

"Why the sad face?" her dad asked.

Poppy shrugged.

"You never have time to talk to me these days," he
said. "You're always too busy with the other men in
your life."

Poppy looked quizzically at him until the penny
dropped. "You mean Cloud and Chester?"

Mike McKeever stuck out his bottom lip and
nodded sorrowfully. He looked so like Charlie that
she had to giggle.

"You twit," she said fondly. "It's because I love
them more."

"Fair enough. I know when I'm beaten. So I'm
presuming that you've come to find me because you
want something. A new Australian rug or some of
those padded socks Cloud wears when he goes in
Bill's trailer?"

"You mean a New Zealand rug, Dad. And they're
not padded socks, they're travel boots. No, I don't
want anything like that. I need some advice."

Her dad muted the TV. "Fire away."

"If you had to raise a huge amount of money for a
horse sanctuary, what would you do?"

"How much are we talking?"

"Thousands. And it needs to be raised quickly."

"Is this for that place Scarlett got her new pony
from?"

Poppy nodded. "Nethercote'll have to close if Jodie
can't find a way to raise enough money. She's getting
desperate." That was the understatement of the year,
Poppy thought to herself.

Her dad rested his chin on steepled fingers. "Britain

is a country of animal lovers. If people knew her horses were under threat they'd dig deep into their pockets, I'm sure."

"That's the problem. People don't know."

"Well then, she must find a way to tell them."

"But how?"

"She needs publicity and she must think big. She needs to tell her story to the TV and newspapers. The money'll come rolling in, I guarantee it."

"But no-one's going to be interested in a tiny horse rescue place in Devon, Dad."

"That's where you've got to think smart. Jodie needs a hook to draw the journalists in. An animal with a tragic back story that'll grab the headlines."

Poppy pictured the real-life magazines her old friend Tory enjoyed with a cup of tea and a slice of Battenberg. There was no doubt Jodie could make a few quid selling her story. *How I smuggled stolen phones into prison to save my horses.* But Poppy didn't think any public relations guru worth their salt would recommend resorting to that particular course of action.

"Every horse at Nethercote has a tragic back story, Dad. That's why they're there."

"Point taken. A tragic *out-of-the-ordinary* back story. You'll think of something, Poppy. You've lived with your old dad long enough to know what makes the news."

It was true, Poppy thought. But her dad was a war correspondent. He covered conflicts in the Middle East. Proper weighty crises and catastrophes in which lives were lost and worlds turned upside down. Stories that newsreaders read with solemn voices, not the light and fluffy news items which ended the bulletins, leaving viewers with a happy heart, their faith in humankind restored.

"So if I do find a tragic, *out-of-the-ordinary* back story, can you help me?"

Her dad ruffled her hair. "'Course I can, sweetheart. I went to journalism college with the producer of Spotlight. I'm sure I can pull in a favour or two. But the story needs to stand up."

Poppy gave Magpie a last chuck under his chin. "Fair enough. Better get started then, hadn't I?"

CHAPTER 16

Hunched over the laptop at the kitchen table with a notepad and pen beside her, Poppy called up the Nethercote Horse Rescue website and clicked on a tab that said *Our horses*. Jodie had reproduced the photos that she'd used on the display panels at the fete. Kirsty, Mr Darcy and Percy were all there. Poppy even spotted the four white socks and white-splodged nose of Red as a foal, being bottle-fed by a much younger-looking Jodie. Poppy skim-read their stories, looking for a hook that would entice the local television station to send a camera crew to Nethercote. Each one was a litany of human cruelty, neglect and ignorance. But although they made Poppy feel sick to the stomach she knew such back stories were universal the world over. Nothing out of the ordinary there.

Sighing, Poppy flipped the laptop closed and stared out of the window, hoping for an epiphany. But the harder she tried to think, the emptier her mind became. Caroline came in from the garden and began washing lettuce for their dinner. Her dad wandered by in search of his reading glasses. Magpie rubbed against her legs before settling into Freddie's bed by the range, the feline equivalent of a self-satisfied smirk on his whiskered face. Still Poppy's mind remained stubbornly blank.

Her reverie was broken when Charlie bowled in like a mini hurricane.

"Can I have a biscuit, Mum?" he called, his hand already in the tin.

"Just one. Dinner won't be long," said Caroline, taking a quiche out of the oven.

Biscuit. The word reverberated around Poppy's head like one of those tiny silver orbs in a pinball machine. Charlie rammed a ginger biscuit in his mouth and crunched noisily. Biscuit. Poppy clapped her hand to her head and Charlie and Caroline looked at her inquiringly.

"I'm so stupid! The answer's been there all along!" Poppy flung her chair back and hugged her brother. "You're a genius, Charlie. An absolute, utter genius!"

Charlie's eyes widened in surprise. "Usually you think I'm an annoying idiot."

"Not today, little brother. Today you are the cleverest person I know. A proper mastermind. Right, I need to see Dad."

He was in the lounge reading the paper. He peered over his glasses as she plonked herself on the sofa.

"I've found an *out-of-the-ordinary* back story," she announced. "What if there was a pony at Nethercote who'd been airlifted by helicopter from the top of a tower block where he'd been kept alive on vegetable peelings, scraps of bread and rainwater?"

Her dad folded the newspaper. "I'd say that was

pretty *out-of-the-ordinary*."

"Caroline said this pony had even been on the news when he was rescued. So if his new home was under threat because of a lack of money, that might make headlines, right?"

"I'd say so," said her dad. "And this pony actually exists, does it?"

Poppy pictured Biscuit, the white spots on his chestnut coat like snowflakes as he snoozed in the daisies. His story wasn't on the Nethercote website, and in her desperation she'd completely forgotten him. "Yes, he definitely exists. So will you phone your friend at Spotlight?"

Her dad was already reaching for his mobile. Poppy chewed a nail as she listened to the one-sided conversation. After what seemed like an age he hung up.

"You're lucky - it's the silly season and they're scratching around for news. They're sending a crew around first thing in the morning. Unless something else breaks it'll be top item on tomorrow's programme. With a fair wind and a bit of luck it'll be picked up by the nationals and those donations will come flooding in."

Poppy hugged her dad. "Thank you, thank you, thank you," she gabbled into his lambswool sweater. "You don't know how much this means."

"No problem, sweetheart. You'd better go and tell Jodie the good news."

Poppy grabbed a slice of quiche and went to catch Cloud. If she cut across the moor it was only about three miles to Nethercote. The Spotlight reporter was due at half nine the following morning. She had to convince Jodie that the interview was the right thing to do. That the publicity it would attract would raise enough money to keep the rescue centre afloat. But, most importantly, Poppy had to talk Jodie out of her plan to smuggle the mobile phones into the prison. Poppy had a feeling that would be the hardest task.

Cloud cantered across the moor, jumping a low stone wall with ease and flying over a small stream. Emotions churned in Poppy's stomach like a witch's potion in a steaming cauldron. Love for her pony. Terror she could lose him. Anxiety about the conversation that lay ahead. And a glimmer of hope that if she could change Jodie's mind, she stood a chance of making everything alright.

Cloud looked around with interest as they walked up the Nethercote drive.

"This is where your new buddy Red used to live," Poppy told him, trying to keep her tone light and her breathing steady. But the waver in her voice gave away her nerves.

Jodie's Land Rover wasn't parked in its usual place. Poppy rang the bell by the tack room but no-one came. Perhaps Jodie was in one of the paddocks. Poppy led Cloud past the stables. His eyes rolled and his nostrils flared in mock horror as the rescue horses watched them walk by.

"It's alright, silly," Poppy said, stroking his neck. "They won't hurt you."

Jodie wasn't in the paddocks either. Poppy checked her watch. Half past six. Time was running out. She knocked at the back door. Inside a radio was playing pop music. She knocked again, harder this time. A door slammed and heels clicked on a stone floor. Jodie's mum appeared, a lipstick in one hand and a handbag in the other. Bracelets jangled on her wrists and her hair had been newly blow dried.

Poppy took a deep breath. "Sorry to bother you but is Jodie in?"

"She isn't, I'm afraid. Disappeared about an hour ago. Didn't even stay for her dinner, the little minx." Her voice was indignant.

"Do you know where she's gone? I really need to speak to her."

Jodie's mum looked cagey. "No idea."

"When will she be back?"

"I don't know, love. I'm not her keeper. Look, I'm late for work. Can I leave her a message?"

Poppy dithered. Could she confide in Jodie's mum? Cloud shifted his weight and nudged Poppy in the back. Jodie's mum looked at her watch and frowned.

Poppy made a snap decision she hoped she wouldn't live to regret.

CHAPTER 17

The air was close and alive with the hum of a million biting insects and the sun was disappearing over the horizon as they arrived home. Poppy untacked Cloud and sponged the sweaty patch under his saddle. Once she'd turned him out with Chester she mindlessly swept the yard until her back ached and sweat trickled down her forehead and between her shoulder blades.

When she could sweep no more she leant on the gate and watched the pony and donkey doze. Every now and then one of them would twitch and shift their weight. Poppy was always dreaming about them. Did they ever dream of her? More likely their dreams were filled with newly-cut hay, sweet spring grass and carrots. Lots of carrots.

She blew them a kiss and headed indoors, where her dad and Caroline were in the lounge watching television. Poppy slumped on the sofa.

"OK sweetheart? Was Jodie pleased?" said Caroline.

"Yes," Poppy said. She kept her eyes glued to the screen so Caroline couldn't read her face.

"Where's Charlie?"

"Just gone up to bed. He's desperate to come over to Nethercote and watch the filming tomorrow. He's hoping they'll interview him as a concerned animal lover. D'you think Jodie would mind?"

Poppy shrugged. "Probably not."

Her mobile beeped. She checked the message.

I've made the call. It's over to you.

"Scarlett?" Caroline asked.

Poppy nodded. Did it count as a lie if she didn't actually articulate it? "She wants me to go over and watch a film. Is that OK?"

"As long as you're back by ten. And make sure you take your phone."

Poppy tapped out a reply and shoved the phone back in her pocket. For better or worse, the first part of her hastily-devised plan was in place.

Poppy's bike was leaning up against the old stone wall around Caroline's vegetable garden, but she walked straight past it and headed for the tack room. Pedal power was no match for horse power in situations like this. She fixed her dad's head torch to her hat and grabbed Cloud's saddle and bridle.

The Connemara showed no surprise when she let herself into the paddock, as if night-time hacks were an everyday occurrence. Poppy glanced nervously towards the house as the gate clicked shut behind her, but the blind in the kitchen was drawn. As long as she was back by ten her parents would be none the wiser.

Something dark swooped in front of her face and she flinched, but it was only one of the bats that had made a home in the rafters of the barn. She led Cloud through the gate and jumped into the saddle.

The setting sun had turned the rippled mass of altocumulus cloud such a vivid shade of fiery orange that it resembled molten lava. Beneath the sky the moss-green moor stretched before them unremittingly, the vast expanse broken only by rocky granite outcrops and the occasional sheep.

Behind her, Riverdale was bathed in tangerine light. Poppy pictured her brother, tucked up in bed, his thumb in his mouth and Magpie curled in a ball by his feet, snoring gently; the television turned down low as her dad and Caroline chatted about their day; Freddie, fast asleep in his basket by the range, his beetle-black nose twitching as he dreamed his doggy dreams. The urge to turn back and join them was so strong Poppy almost succumbed to it. This was Jodie's mess. Why should it be up to her to sort it out? Jodie had made her bed. Let her lie in it.

But Poppy knew it was too late. She'd set off a chain of events and had no choice but to see it through. She had to do right by the Nethercote horses. She just hoped her plan worked. And if it didn't....

Anxiety gnawing at her insides, Poppy clicked her tongue and asked for a canter. Cloud needed no encouragement and sprang forwards. He was fizzing with nervous energy, his neck arched and his tail high. Poppy licked her lips and tried to slow her racing heartbeat. The last thing she wanted was for her pony to pick up on her tension. The Connemara lengthened his stride until he was galloping flat out. She sighed. It seemed he already had.

"Hey boy, not so fast. There's a long way to go," she soothed. She tried checking him but the reins slipped through her clammy fingers. A dark stain of sweat was spreading across his neck and shoulders and his head was tucked into his chest. Poppy sat down in the saddle, kept her legs firmly against Cloud's sides and gave a firm, even pull with both reins.

"Whoa," she murmured. Cloud flicked back his ears and finally slowed his stride. Poppy checked him again and he broke into a fast, unbalanced trot.

"Steady," she said, sitting for a few uncomfortable strides until she was able to ease him into a walk. She bent down and stroked his neck.

Poppy loosened the reins, relieved to have brought him back under control. He had never taken off like that before. She kept up a stream of chatter as they crossed the moor, hoping her voice would keep him calm. The sun was sinking below the horizon and the sky had darkened to the grey of a stormy sea. By Poppy's reckoning they were over halfway. With any luck they'd reach the cottage before darkness fell. She'd hoped for a clear night but no such luck. She'd have to rely on her pony's instinct and the beam of the head torch to guide them home.

They passed a small herd of Dartmoor ponies grazing by the side of a stream. A roan mare with a bay foal at foot lifted her head and whinnied. Cloud skittered to the left and Poppy clamped her legs to his sides and tightened her reins.

After a mile or so Cloud finally began to settle. Poppy let the reins slip through her fingers so he could stretch his neck. As she relaxed into his long, loping walk her mind began to wander. Humming tunelessly, she scratched a mosquito bite on her arm and played with a hank of the Connemara's mane. She was so preoccupied she didn't see the flash of iridescent green until too late. As they approached a

107

clump of gorse bushes a male pheasant squawked in alarm and swooped in front of them, its speckled conker and black wings outstretched. Cloud boggled and leapt about three feet into the air, throwing Poppy out of the saddle. For a split second, as she teetered on the brink, she thought she might save herself. But the saddle slipped and with it went her balance. The ground rushed towards her as fast as a fairground helter-skelter and Poppy landed heavily, her right leg buckling underneath her. She gasped as she felt her ankle pop. Intense pain shot up her leg. And then everything went black.

CHAPTER 18

Roused from semi-consciousness by a draught of warm air, Poppy reached for the alarm clock on her bedside table. When her hand came into contact with wiry grass and a small slab of cold granite her eyes snapped open. Cloud's nose was a few inches from her own. He blew softly into her face, as if he was trying to wake her. That explained the warm air at least.

Totally disorientated, Poppy looked around her, wondering if she'd fallen asleep in the paddock again. She sat up groggily and winced at the stabbing pain in her leg. Cloud whickered and nuzzled her neck, his liquid brown eyes dark with concern. She tried to piece together what had happened. Bit by bit she remembered: the text, the made-up visit to see Scarlett, the dash across the moor to the tumbledown cottage, the pheasant...

"Pesky pheasant!" Poppy muttered, attempting to stand. But the searing pain took her breath away and she collapsed on the grass again. Gingerly, she peeled down her sock. Her ankle had ballooned in size, the skin around it stretched and puffy. Her heart sank. How was she ever going to reach Witch Cottage now?

As if sensing her thoughts Cloud gave her a gentle nudge. Poppy swallowed back tears. "I can't ride you, Cloud. There's no way I can stand to get on. And I can't walk a single step. I'll have to call Caroline and Dad. I have no other choice."

She slid her phone out of her back pocket and groaned. No signal. Not even one measly bar. She threw it onto the grass in frustration. Cloud sniffed it cautiously, his nostrils flared, and took a step back.

"Don't leave me!" Poppy cried, the gravity of her situation beginning to sink in. It was almost nine o'clock at night, she was in the middle of the moor with a useless leg and an equally useless phone. Jodie was about to throw her life away and there was nothing Poppy could do to stop her. Her shoulders sagged in defeat.

Cloud must have registered the desperation in her voice, because he walked forward and rubbed his head against her, as if to say *Don't worry, I'll stick around*. She pressed her face against his warm cheek.

"I can do this," she told him. Heaving herself upright she gathered Cloud's reins, rested her left hand on his withers and grabbed the stirrup. But her right ankle was too feeble and she crumpled to the ground. "Oh Cloud, what am I going to do?"

The Connemara pawed the ground and sank to his knees with a grunt.

"Don't roll, you'll squash your saddle!"

But Cloud didn't roll. He lay down beside her and nudged her hip.

Was he lying down in sympathy? Poppy knew

horses were empathetic but this was ridiculous. Maybe he'd twisted his leg when he'd spooked, too.

"Have you hurt yourself?" she cried.

Cloud nudged her again. Poppy leant against him, reassured by his solid bulk. She often lay down with him in the stable. She'd once read that if a horse even let someone near them while they were lying down it was a sign of trust. It had made her feel slightly superior that Cloud was so relaxed with her that he sometimes dozed off with his head in her lap. She'd watched videos on YouTube of horses who'd been trained to lie down on command. Some even lay down so their riders could mount them from their wheelchairs.

Suddenly a thought popped into her head. She knew from Caitlyn's diary that she'd started teaching Cloud tricks. Had she taught him to lie down so she could get on from the ground? It seemed unbelievable but it was worth a try. There were no other options.

Poppy shuffled on her bottom to Cloud's saddle, gathered the reins again and grabbed a handful of mane.

"Are you OK with this?" she asked him. He looked completely at ease. She took a deep breath, put her weight on her left knee and hauled her right leg over. Once she was sitting in the saddle she touched his withers and held on tightly as he scrambled to his feet.

Poppy threw her arms around his neck. "You clever, clever boy!"

Leaving her swollen foot dangling she crossed the right stirrup over the saddle so it didn't bump against his side and clicked her tongue, her optimism restored.

"Come on Cloud. We have a disaster to avert!"

Poppy saw the headlights of Jodie's Land Rover before they left the inky blackness of the conifers. It looked as though they had arrived in the nick of time. Jodie, wearing a dark baseball cap and riding gloves, was cramming dozens of phones into a large black holdall.

"Jodie! It's me, Poppy."

Jodie spun around. Her face, caught in the beam of Poppy's head torch, was twisted with fury and fear.

"What the hell are you doing here?"

"I've come to stop you."

"Too late."

"It isn't! You don't have to do this!"

"I do," Jodie said grimly.

"But I've found another way to raise the money!"

"Yeah, right."

"I really have. The BBC is sending a camera crew to Nethercote in the morning."

"*What?*"

"They're going to do a story on your appeal."

"There is no appeal."

"There will be by the morning," Poppy said. "You're going to set one up on your website tonight."

Jodie turned back to the holdall. "It'd be a complete waste of time. There are too many animal sanctuaries out there asking for money. I've already told you that."

"None of the others will be top item on tomorrow's news. My dad's had a word with the producer. She loves Biscuit's story. She's going to use old footage of him being carried down by the helicopter, and they're going to interview you about him and the appeal.

Once people see the great work you're doing the donations will come flooding in!"

Jodie tucked a loose strand of hair behind her ear. Poppy noticed the slightest tremor in her fingers.

"Didn't it occur to you to ask me first?" Jodie said coldly.

Poppy was silent.

"No, I didn't think so. I'm not doing it. I don't need to. By this time tomorrow I'll have enough in the bank to keep Nethercote running for a year."

"But it's all organised!"

Jodie shoved the last few phones into the bag and yanked the zip closed. "Well, you've wasted your time. Now beggar off and leave me to it."

"You'll get caught," Poppy said.

"You sound like my mother. How many times do I have to say it? I will not get caught. Everything is planned. So if you'll excuse me, there's somewhere I need to be."

"Your dad won't be there."

Jodie flung the holdall in the back of the Land Rover and slammed the door. "What are you wittering about?"

Poppy took a deep breath. "He won't be lowering the rope. He's in solitary confinement."

"*What?*" Jodie said again.

"The Governor knows what your dad's planning. He had a tip off. There are four prison officers in his cell and police on the ground waiting for the phones to arrive."

"You've grassed us up?" Jodie hissed.

"Not me. It was your mum. But no-one knows it's you bringing the phones. She told them it was some lowlife your dad met in prison."

"And that makes it alright does it?"

"She reckons he'll end up serving extra time. But that it's a small price to pay in the circumstances."

Poppy thought it wise not repeat Jodie's mum's actual words, that he could go to hell for all she cared. Instead she said, "Your mum said he'd be happy as long as you and the horses were OK."

Jodie leant against the Land Rover, her head bowed. "If that's true, what am I going to do with the phones?"

Poppy glanced at the cottage. "Put them back in the attic. I'll call the police in a couple of days and say I've found them. It won't matter if my fingerprints are all over them. There'll be nothing to link them to you."

"What about the gang who stole them. They know who I am," Jodie said.

"But they're hardly going to hand themselves in, are they?"

Sensing Jodie waver Poppy pressed home her advantage. "What would Cait tell you to do, if she was here? Would she want her best friend to break the law and risk going to prison? It's the last thing she'd want."

Jodie was silent. After what seemed like an eternity she edged over to Cloud and stroked his head. Poppy felt a pounding in her chest and realised she'd stopped breathing.

"She'd tell me I was nuts to even consider it," said Jodie finally.

Poppy sent a silent missive of thanks to Caitlyn.

"So you'll do it? The interview and everything?"

"You really think it'll work?"

The beam of the head torch bobbed like a yo-yo as Poppy nodded. "It'll work. I promise."

CHAPTER 19

"So, are you going to give me a hand with these phones or what?" said Jodie.

Poppy reddened. "I can't get off. I fell off Cloud and busted my ankle on the way over."

Jodie raised her eyebrows. "Is it broken?"

"I don't think so. I can still wiggle my toes, although it really hurts. I think it's just a sprain."

"How did you get back on?"

"Well, that's the funny thing," said Poppy. "Did you and Caitlyn teach Cloud and Nero tricks that last summer?"

Jodie hooted with laughter. "I tried to. Nero was hopeless. But Cloud was a quick learner, weren't you boy? Cait taught him to give her a kiss and take a bow, that kind of thing."

"Did she teach him to lie down?"

Jodie's forehead creased. "Not that I remember. But it was so long ago. D'you want me to go home and get the trailer?"

"No, we'll take it easy. We'll be fine. But will you be

OK to put the phones back in the attic?"

"Do I have an option?" Jodie's tone was sardonic, but she dragged the hold-all out of the back of the Land Rover and hefted it onto her shoulder.

"I'll see you tomorrow," Poppy said.

Jodie held her hand in a mock salute. As Cloud plunged back into the conifers Poppy glanced back. In the beam of the Land Rover's headlights she could just make out the older girl disappearing through the door of the cottage. Poppy ran her hand along Cloud's neck and allowed herself a smile.

"D'you know, Cloud? I think it's going to be alright."

It was only when they were almost home that she realised she had overlooked one small but crucial problem. How on earth was she going to explain her sprained ankle to her parents?

"So you decided to ride Cloud to Scarlett's - even though it was pitch dark - and fell off on the way home when he shied at a sheep?" Caroline asked, her eyebrows raised.

"Er, yes. That's right." Poppy hopped over to the gate and rested her bad ankle on the bottom bar. Her nose would be as long as Pinocchio's if she carried on lying like this.

"We'd better take you to minor injuries first thing to check it's not a fracture," said her dad.

"I can't miss the filming!" Poppy cried. "I've promised Jodie I'll be there. Honestly, I'm fine. The swelling's gone down already." She rotated her ankle, hiding her grimace behind her long fringe. "See?"

Caroline sighed. "Alright. But you won't be able to ride. I'll drive you."

Poppy hopped over to her stepmum and gave her a hug. Caroline ruffled her hair.

"Come on, Hopalong Cassidy. It's getting late and you should be in bed."

Poppy screwed up her face. "What did you call me?"

"Hopalong Cassidy. He was a cowboy in the old Western films my grandad used to love. Hopalong had a grey horse, too, though he was called Topper, if my memory serves me right."

Lying in bed, her ankle resting on two pillows and Magpie nestled in the crook of her arm, Poppy Googled Hopalong Cassidy.

"Wikipedia says he was often called upon to intercede when dishonest characters took advantage of honest citizens," she told the cat, who yawned widely, showing two rows of tiny incisors.

Poppy turned off the iPad and tickled Magpie's chin. "We've more in common than a gammy leg."

Over breakfast Poppy checked Nethercote's website. Jodie had been busy. On the home page was a huge banner urging people to support the rescue centre's new appeal. Under a photo of Jodie with her arm around Biscuit's neck was an open letter. Poppy's toast grew cold on her plate as she read:

'Hi, I'm Jodie Morgan, and I run Nethercote Horse Rescue.
I want to take this opportunity to tell you a little bit about us and the work we do.
Nethercote was founded by my dad, Alan Morgan, ten years ago. Dad always loved horses and opening a rescue centre was his life's dream.
Dad never once turned a horse away. He gave them all

a second chance.

Horses like Biscuit, our most famous resident here at Nethercote, who was rescued by helicopter from the roof of a high rise block of flats. We try and rehome as many horses as possible, but I have promised Biscuit that he has a home here for the rest of his days.

Five years ago Dad left the running of Nethercote to me. I was fifteen and still at school. Running a rescue centre wasn't my dream - I wanted to be a famous showjumper - but I owed it to the horses to carry on. A job like this is a vocation. Seeing a pony that arrived skinny and terrified go off to his new home sleek and confident makes all the hard work worthwhile.

But the last few years have been tough. Really tough. Money has been tight and fundraising takes up precious time better spent rescuing, rehabilitating and rehoming our horses and ponies.

This summer we reached crisis point at Nethercote. Costs for hay and feed have soared and donations have plummeted. Without financial help we won't be able to pay the winter feed bill, let alone meet ongoing veterinary and farrier costs. What will happen to the horses, you may well ask. The truth is, I don't know. So we have launched Biscuit's Appeal, to raise enough money to enable us to carry on caring for the horses other people have forgotten. If you are able to help, please donate using the link below.

Every penny counts: £5 will buy a bale of hay, £10 will buy a sack of food, £20 will pay for the farrier to trim a pony's feet and £80 will buy him a new set of shoes.

So, you see, your help really can make all the difference to Biscuit and his friends here at Nethercote. Thank

you for listening in our hour of need.
Yours, Jodie

Poppy swallowed. Jodie's letter was heartfelt and emotive and, as if that wasn't enough to get people reaching for their chequebooks, there was a blurry photo in the bottom right hand corner of Biscuit being winched to safety from the tower block in the Midlands. The appaloosa was a bag of skin and bones, a far cry from the plump, contented pony he was now.

Charlie bounded in, his hair as tousled as a bird's nest, Freddie hot on his heels. He skidded to a halt when he saw Poppy.

"No tablets at the breakfast table!"

"I'm not playing games, I'm reading. The BBC film crew is coming today and I need to check the website so I can give Jodie some advice on handling the media, if you must know," Poppy told him officiously.

"Doesn't look like she needs it," said Caroline, reading over Poppy's shoulder. "I'd say she was pretty much on message already."

"Yes, well, I did brief her last night. I mean, yesterday afternoon." Poppy felt her cheeks redden. Hoping Caroline hadn't noticed, she picked up her plate and hobbled over to the sink. The swelling in her ankle had gone down overnight but it was still too tender to take her full weight.

"What time do we need to go?" Caroline asked.

"They're coming at half past nine so if we leave at eight thirty I can make sure Jodie's ready."

"Can me and Freddie come? They might want to do a vod pod," said Charlie.

Poppy gazed at him in exasperation. "A *what?*"

"You know, when they ask members of the public what they think about something. They might do a vod pod about how important it is to save the ponies."

Caroline laughed. "He means vox pop. I suppose it wouldn't do any harm. As long as you promise not to get under everybody's feet. You don't mind, do you Poppy?"

"I won't be annoying, I promise." Charlie smiled beseechingly at his sister.

"Oh alright, if you must. But if you ruin everything by messing up a shot or something I will have no option but to kill you."

"I understand," he nodded earnestly, before giving a fist pump and bowling back out of the kitchen, Freddie still at his feet.

Poppy sighed. Brothers!

CHAPTER 20

Jodie looked as if she'd only managed to snatch a couple of hours' sleep. Purple shadows darkened her eyes like shading on a pencil portrait and her face was pale. But she greeted the McKeevers with a cheerful smile and made a great fuss of Freddie, who promptly rolled on the ground with his legs in the air offering his belly to be tickled.

"Is there anything we can do?" Caroline asked.

"I've just got the yard to sweep and Biscuit to groom. I wanted him looking his best," said Jodie.

"Poppy can take care of Biscuit and I'll sweep the yard. You go and get yourself ready."

Jodie smiled gratefully and disappeared inside. Poppy tied Biscuit outside his stable and set to work with a body brush. The appaloosa was already beginning to lose his summer coat and Poppy sneezed violently as she was enveloped in a cloud of horse hair. Catching a whiff of the Polos in her back pocket, Biscuit nibbled at her jeans until Poppy relented. He wolfed two from her open palm as if he hadn't been

121

fed for a week, which, Poppy reflected, had probably been the case when he'd been tethered at the top of the high rise. It was little wonder he was a guzzle guts when a decent meal back then would have been a pile of potato scrapings and a couple of slices of mouldy bread. Poppy shuddered, then peeled another couple of mints from the pack.

She was brushing out the tangles in the appaloosa's tail when Jodie's mum tottered across the yard in the highest wedge shoes Poppy had ever seen. She laid a hand on Poppy's arm.

"Thank you for everything you did yesterday, Poppy. You don't know how grateful I am. I've got my old Jodie back."

"I was glad to help. I don't think deep down she wanted to do it, she just felt she had no option."

Jodie's mum's lips thinned. "Her father should never have put her in that position. What was he thinking?"

Poppy considered this. She would lay down her life for Cloud. She could understand why Alan Morgan had been prepared to take such a risk. But it didn't make it right.

The back door banged shut and Jodie appeared, wearing a clean, if a little creased, red Nethercote tee-shirt, navy jodhpurs and black riding boots. Despite her wan face she looked upbeat, as though a great weight had been lifted from her shoulders.

"Are you ready for your moment of fame?" Caroline asked.

Jodie grimaced. "My stomach's churning, my mouth is as dry as sandpaper and I've absolutely no idea what I'm going to say. But otherwise, yes, bring it on."

"We can have a run-through if you like," Poppy said shyly. "I can pretend I'm the reporter and ask you some questions."

"And I'll be the cameraman," said Charlie, sticking an imaginary camera in Jodie's face.

"Anything that'll help."

Poppy and Charlie had watched their dad on the news enough times to know how to conduct a television interview and they spent the next ten minutes grilling Jodie until she was word perfect. They had hardly drawn breath when a spotless black BMW pulled up at the gate.

"Oh God, they're here!" Jodie cried, smoothing her hair self-consciously.

"You'll be fine," Caroline told her. "Forget the camera's there and just be yourself."

A man in his thirties dressed in a cream linen suit and reeking of a spicy, pungent aftershave introduced himself as reporter Ben Byrne. He shook everyone's hand and gave Biscuit a tentative pat while his cameraman, a smiley girl called Pippa, fiddled with her camera.

"We'll do the interview first, then Pippa will get some general shots of the yard and we'll finish with a piece to camera," Ben told them.

Biscuit watched with interest as Ben held out a microphone and said, "Can you give us your name for the level?"

Jodie cleared her throat. "Um. Jodie Morgan."

"Great. And can you spell your name for the tape?"

"J-O-I-D. Sorry," she said, shaking her head and shooting a desperate look at the others. Poppy gave her an encouraging smile and Caroline mouthed, "You'll be fine."

"J-O-D-I-E-M-O-R-G-A-N."

"Wonderful. Let's get started."

123

After the first couple of questions Jodie's nerves vanished and she talked animatedly about the rescue horses. Ben asked her about Biscuit and his condition when he'd arrived at Nethercote.

"The vet said he'd never make it. But Biscuit's a fighter. In fact he's as stubborn as I am. He refused to give up." Jodie scratched the pony's forehead and he gave her an affectionate nudge. "I promised him that if he pulled through he would never have to leave. And now I'm not sure I'll be able to keep that promise," she said, her voice thick with emotion.

Poppy, who was standing behind the camera, could see that Pippa had zoomed in on Jodie's face, catching the single tear that slid down her cheek.

Interview over, they took Pippa on a tour of the rescue centre so she could get shots of horses grazing contentedly in the paddocks and looking over their stable doors.

"Jodie can send you some of the before pictures," said Poppy, thinking of the photos of horses with matted coats, hollow necks, overgrown hooves and bony rumps that had had such an impact on her at the summer fete.

When Pippa had finished they returned to the yard.

"We don't need you for this bit, Jodie. I'm going to do a piece to camera telling everyone about the appeal," said Ben.

"Why don't you hold Biscuit while you're doing it?" Pippa suggested.

Poppy untied the appaloosa and handed his leadrope to Ben, who took it gingerly.

"It's alright. He won't bite," Jodie laughed.

Poppy darted forwards and brushed the reporter's linen jacket. He looked at her in bemusement.

"Just a bit of fluff," she said, retreating to where Caroline, Charlie and Freddie were watching the proceedings.

Ben smoothed down his hair, glanced at his notebook and switched on his mike. Pippa squinted through the eyepiece of her camera and gave him the thumbs up. He gripped Biscuit's leadrope tightly and gave the camera a dazzling smile.

"Biscuit and his equine friends here at Nethercote Horse Rescue have been given a second chance by Jodie Morgan. But unless the rescue centre can raise more funds their future is uncertain..."

While everyone else was watching the reporter, Poppy's eyes were trained on Biscuit. *Come on*, she willed him silently. *You can do it.*

Ben was wrapping up his piece to camera when the gelding suddenly raised his head and sniffed the wind. He gave a comedy snort and turned towards the reporter. There was a glint in his eye as he gave Ben a purposeful nudge and started nibbling at his jacket. Momentarily thrown, Ben raised his eyebrows and shrugged theatrically. Biscuit, still picking at Ben's jacket, breathed in a lungful of the reporter's tangy aftershave, turned to face the camera and curled his top lip as if he was laughing his speckled head off.

Poppy held her breath as she watched Pippa focus on the appaloosa's yellow teeth. Beside her Charlie stifled a giggle. Poppy elbowed him in the ribs and held her finger to her lips. This was television gold. They'd never re-create it if they had to do a second take.

Ben had thrown his head back and was also roaring with laughter. "And with that, it's back to you in the studio," he spluttered, as Biscuit rolled his eyes at the camera and sneezed explosively all over the reporter's cream linen suit.

"That horse is a comic genius. You ought to get him an agent," said Ben, as he helped Pippa heft the camera into the boot of the BMW.

"Comic genius? A total delinquent more like. I'm sorry about your jacket," Jodie said for the umpteenth time.

"No worries. I'll get it dry cleaned on expenses."

"What time will Jodie be on the news?" asked Charlie.

Ben checked his watch. "Half past one and again at six thirty."

"And you'll include the link so people can donate if they want to?" Poppy checked.

He nodded. "I think people will be falling over themselves to help once they see Biscuit in action. He's a star in the making. I was well and truly upstaged," he said ruefully.

"I bet I look like a complete and utter loser," grumbled Jodie, as they settled in Nethercote's living room to watch the lunchtime bulletin.

"You don't need to worry. People'll be more interested in Biscuit than you," said Charlie kindly.

"Thanks - I think."

Poppy felt a flutter of nerves as the titles came up and the familiar soundtrack began to play. She was the one who had convinced Jodie this would work. What if it didn't? If no-one supported Biscuit's Appeal Jodie would be right back at square one. Actually worse than that. Poppy had already scuppered her money-making plan to smuggle phones into Dartmoor prison.

A willowy presenter with an improbably unlined forehead and immaculately coiffured hair swept into a chignon was sitting on a red sofa. She shuffled some papers on her lap and looked up as the titles ended. Poppy's mind wandered as the presenter read the headlines with a practised smile.

"- but first we go to a Devon horse sanctuary that needs your help. Ben Byrne reports."

The camera cut to the main paddock where the plump, sleek Nethercote horses grazed serenely under a canopy of ancient oak trees, and then cut again to Ben's interview with Jodie, which was peppered with some of the less graphic photographs of the rescue horses. Jodie scowled when the camera zoomed in on the tear rolling down her cheek.

"Why did they have to show that?"

"It makes great television," said Caroline.

Poppy's phone buzzed with a text from Scarlett.

OMG Poppy, you need to turn on the telly like NOW!! Jodie's on Spotlight!

I know, Poppy tapped back. *I fixed it.*

I'm recording it so I can show Red later.

You're nuts. He's not a human you know.

Yes he is!! Hey wait a minute, what d'you mean you fixed it?

Poppy grinned to herself. *It's a long story*, she tapped back. *Tell you later.*

Ben was now with Biscuit, doing his piece to camera.

"What I don't get is why he started eating Ben's jacket," said Jodie.

Poppy absentmindedly fingered the packet of Polos in her jeans. She'd slipped one into the reporter's pocket when she'd pretended to dust off the piece of fluff, hoping that Biscuit would sniff it out. What she hadn't bargained for was the potency of Ben's aftershave, which had prompted the gelding to flash his teeth to the world.

"I never knew horses could laugh until Biscuit did that," said Charlie.

"He's not laughing. It's called the flehmen response. I read it in my pony magazine," Poppy said. "When horses smell something they're not sure about they curl back their upper lips and breathe in with their nostrils closed. It must have been Ben's aftershave."

"I'm not surprised Biscuit didn't like it. It was totally yuck," Charlie said.

The appaloosa's reaction to the reporter looked even funnier on television. Even the presenter was hooting with laughter by the time Ben handed back to the studio.

"And they've remembered to include the link to the website," said Caroline. "I'd say that was a job well done."

CHAPTER 21

Slivers of sunlight stole through a gap in Poppy's curtains and danced on her closed eyelids with dogged determination, willing her to wake up. She yawned, stretched her arms above her head and rotated her bad ankle. Relieved to discover it was well and truly on the mend, she reached for her phone and tried to open the Nethercote website.

Large red letters told her the server application was unavailable. She hit refresh but the page failed to load. Poppy stabbed at the refresh button a couple more times before texting Jodie.

What's happened to the website? It won't load.

Her phone beeped within seconds.

Damn thing's crashed. No idea why.

A smile crept across Poppy's face. She had a sneaking suspicion. And if she was right it could only be good news for Nethercote. She Googled the rescue centre and half a dozen stories appeared. Biscuit had made headlines in the Daily Mail, the Daily Mirror and even a couple of the broadsheets. A

clip of Spotlight's news item on YouTube had been
viewed just over nine thousand times. Poppy checked
the Daily Mail's Facebook page. The story had been
shared by almost three hundred people. She typed
#Biscuit into Google. Dozens more tweets, posts and
Instagram tags popped up. She sighed with
satisfaction. Her plan had worked. She was a public
relations genius. Biscuit the Laughing Horse had gone
viral.

Poppy cantered Cloud across the field to Ashworthy,
humming happily to herself. Caroline had taken a bit
of convincing that her ankle was OK to ride but had
finally relented when Poppy had promised she'd hack
out with Scarlett and Red. Soon the two girls were
heading out across the moor.

"The YouTube views went up by almost fifteen
hundred in the time it took me to eat my breakfast,"
Poppy told Scarlett.

"That's amazing. But no-one will be able to donate
if the website's crashed."

"It's back up and running now. Jodie said donations
have already reached twenty eight thousand but
they're still pouring in. Channel 5 is sending a reporter
over this afternoon and ITN is doing an outside
broadcast from Nethercote this evening."

"Better tell Jodie to wear lots of perfume," Scarlett
said.

"I can't imagine her smothering herself in Christian
Dior, can you? She's more like us. Prefers Eau de
Horse," Poppy giggled.

Scarlett ran her hand along Red's neck. The gelding's
chestnut coat gleamed.

"Did you give him another bath this morning?"

"Just a quick one to get rid of his stable stains. It's quite exhausting, keeping him spotless," Scarlett admitted.

Poppy looked down at the grass stains on Cloud's front legs. "Why don't you chill out? A few stable stains aren't going to kill him."

"I know." Scarlett was silent for a while. Then, as they skirted the base of the Riverdale tor, she said, "Where are we going to go?"

"We need to ride to Witch Cottage. There's something I need to do."

Scarlett groaned. "But I hate it there, you know that."

"It's just a derelict old cottage, Scar. Stones and mortar. There are no ghosts."

"So why are we going?"

Poppy wondered where to start. She had a feeling that, in her excitement over Red, Scarlett had all but forgotten the existence of the phones Poppy had discovered hidden under the green tarpaulin in the croft's tiny attic. She may have realised that they were the ones stolen from the warehouse in Plymouth. But Poppy knew for certain that she had no clue they had been destined for the prison, and that Jodie had been pivotal in the whole shady enterprise.

Poppy and Scarlett now had to accidentally stumble across the cache of phones, paste on innocent faces and report their find to the police, as Poppy had promised Jodie she would.

"Poppy," Scarlett repeated. "Why do we need to go to Witch Cottage?"

"I'll tell you when we get there."

The warm summer breeze tickled Cloud's silver mane and he snatched at the bit. His excitement was infectious. Poppy felt giddy with relief. As though it was seven o'clock on Christmas morning. Or the first day of the summer holidays. Everything had worked out just fine. Better than fine. Absolutely gobsmackingly brilliantly. And who could have guessed, a week ago, that Nethercote would be saved by an amazing, courageous, laughing horse?

The wiry moorland grass felt springy and perfect for a canter. Poppy kicked Cloud on. Red caught up with the Connemara in a couple of strides and soon the two ponies, one dappled grey, the other the colour of butterscotch, were galloping neck and neck towards Witch Cottage.

As they raced across the moor, their ponies' tails streaming like banners behind them, Poppy imagined Caitlyn and Jodie making the same journey on a warm summer's morning just like this one, their destination a tumbledown cottage with a teardrop-shaped tarn, a catslide roof and secrets woven into its granite walls.

Poppy glanced at her best friend. Scarlett must have sensed her gaze as she turned her head. Her hazel eyes sparkled.

"It feels like we're off on an adventure!" she cried.

Poppy, who was crouching low over Cloud's neck as he covered the ground in long, easy strides, couldn't help but agree. One adventure was over, but she was pretty sure there was another waiting for them, just beyond the vast Dartmoor horizon. And she couldn't wait.

Read on for the first three chapters of Juno's Foal by Amanda Wills

CHAPTER 1

Summer on the Farm

Leah Lindberg was re-arranging her pony books in alphabetical order when her mum marched into her bedroom and ruined her summer.

"Dad and I are flying to the UK for a lecture tour on Monday. You're going to stay with your Aunt Freya while we're away. It's all arranged."

"What?" Leah spluttered, catching a glimpse of herself in her dressing table mirror. Her face had turned as white as her jodhpurs.

"I'm sorry to spring it on you darling, but it was too good an opportunity to turn down." Her mum didn't even have the grace to look abashed.

"I've never met Aunt Freya. She's not even my proper aunt!"

133

"She's your godmother, and you have met her, although you were probably too young to remember. That's why I thought it would be a lovely opportunity to get to know her and the twins."

"The twins?" Leah sat down on her bed with a thump. She'd forgotten about Oscar and Isabella.

"They must be eight now. Only a year younger than you. You'll have a fantastic summer, I promise you."

Leah was about to protest. But her mum had already turned on her heels and disappeared out of the room.

Leah picked her way through the puddles on the rutted track to the riding school and tried to ignore the feeling of gloom that clung to her like a limpet. She'd been looking forward to the summer holidays for weeks, especially after her mum had agreed she could help out at the stables every weekend. Instead she was being sent to her godmother's farm miles away. It wasn't fair.

Her heart gave a little leap when she saw Sparkle tied up outside his stable, his grey head buried in a haynet. She reached in the pocket of her jodhpurs for a carrot and whistled. Sparkle turned his head, saw her and whinnied. Leah flung her arms around his neck and tried not to think about how much she'd miss him.

She jumped when a girl's face appeared over Sparkle's withers. The girl had streaks of mud on her cheeks and so much hay sticking out of her tousled brown hair that she could have passed for a human haynet. Her navy jodhpurs and shirt were covered in dust.

"Hello!" said the girl. "I'm Lisa. Are you Leah?"

Leah nodded and squirmed as Lisa looked her up

and down.

"Sam said you have a lesson at ten. Sparkle's all ready for you."

"Thanks. He looks great." Leah offered Sparkle the carrot and he picked it daintily from her palm. She smiled as his whiskers tickled her fingers, not noticing that Lisa was still staring at her, her eyes wide.

"How on earth do you manage to keep so clean?" Lisa asked.

Leah looked down. Her jodhpurs were freshly-laundered and as white as Sparkle's immaculately-groomed flanks. Her black leather boots were so shiny she could see her face in them. She shrugged. "Not sure. I just do."

"Lucky you. My mum's always giving me grief for being so scruffy. Yesterday she threatened to hose me down before she let me in the house," Lisa laughed. "Sam said you're helping out this summer, too."

Leah's face clouded over. "Not any more. I'm going to stay with my godmother on her farm. I've only just found out."

"That's a shame. Still, summer on a farm sounds like fun. Does she have horses?"

Leah thought hard. She knew Freya had cattle and sheep. She seemed to remember there were chickens, too. But no-one had ever mentioned horses.

"I don't think so," she said glumly. Sparkle nuzzled her pockets. On the other side of the yard Sam, the riding school's owner, was opening the gate into the menage.

"You'd better go or you'll be in trouble. You know how much Sam hates people being late for lessons," Lisa said, reaching for a yard broom.

Leah flashed her a grateful smile. She adjusted the

stirrups, checked Sparkle's girth and swung into the saddle. She gathered her reins and was turning the little grey pony towards the menage when a thought struck her.

"Lisa?"

Lisa stopped sweeping. "What's up?"

"Will you look after Sparkle while I'm away? Make sure he gets lots of attention? I'm going to miss him so much." Leah's eyes prickled with unshed tears. She reached for the handkerchief in her pocket and blew her nose.

"Of course I will. I'll give him a cuddle three times a day and tell him it's from you."

"And a carrot," Leah said with a watery smile. "He loves carrots."

Lisa nodded, stroking Sparkle's soft nose. "Carrots and cuddles. No problem."

Leah's gloom lifted a fraction. At least she was leaving Sparkle in good hands.

CHAPTER 2

Hollow End

Freya and her twins Isabella and Oscar lived on a remote farm a four hour drive from the city where Leah had lived all her life. Freya and Leah's mum had been friends since university but although they talked regularly on the phone they hadn't seen each other for years.

Leah's stomach churned at the thought of spending the entire summer with people she didn't know. What if her godmother was strict and the twins were horrible? There was a photo above the fireplace of Freya holding Leah at her christening. Leah was wearing a white christening gown and a beaming smile, her chubby fists waving at the camera as Freya gazed at her fondly. Her godmother had shoulder-length dark brown hair, wide-set grey eyes and a crinkly smile. Leah had to admit that she didn't look strict, but you never knew.

Her mum caught her studying the photo that evening.

"Don't worry Leah, you'll love Freya," she said. "And if the twins are anything like their mum, you'll love them too."

"Where's their dad?"

"He and Freya divorced about five years ago. That's when she moved to the farm."

"Does she have any horses?"

Her mum sighed. "Life doesn't revolve around horses, Leah."

Leah stuck out her chin. "It does for me."

Two days later Leah was sitting in the back of the car, her suitcase beside her, trying to calm her nerves as the countryside sped past.

"Not long now," said her dad, watching her in the rear-view mirror.

"What time's your plane?" Leah asked.

"Not 'til seven," said her mum.

"Make sure you get seats by the emergency exit," Leah reminded them.

Leah wasn't a pessimist. She just liked to be prepared. She listened to safety talks on planes and ferries and always checked where fire exits were when she visited somewhere new. She knew how to put someone in the recovery position and could list where every single fire extinguisher was kept in her school. Her parents thought it wasn't normal behaviour for a nine-year-old but Leah didn't care. If she was going to be stuck on a plane with engine trouble she wanted to know exactly how to inflate her life-jacket.

"There's the turning," said her dad, pointing to a roughshod lane which looped away to their left. Leah craned her neck to catch a glimpse of the farm. They passed a handpainted sign propped against a weathered five bar gate. Hollow End. Leah shivered in spite of the warmth of the car. It sounded like the end of the world.

The car slowed to a halt outside a rambling wooden farmhouse that had been painted sage green. Leah flicked a speck of fluff from her favourite red shorts and smoothed her hair self-consciously. Before she could undo her seatbelt two rosy-faced children appeared outside her window. One opened the passenger door and the other beckoned her out.

"I'm Oscar," said the boy. "And that's -"

"Isabella," finished the girl. "We've been waiting for you for ages."

Her godmother stepped forward, her tanned face creased in a smile. "And you probably don't remember me, but I'm Freya."

Leah held out her hand politely but Freya ignored her and swept her into a hug. She smelt of newly-cut hay and molasses and her faded checked cotton shirt had been washed so many times it was soft against Leah's cheek.

"Look at you, all grown up! It's been too long."

The twins disappeared into a barn behind them and Leah stood awkwardly while Freya and her parents chatted about the journey. She almost jumped out of her skin when she felt something warm and furry rub against her knee. She looked down to see a ginger farm cat weaving between her legs, purring loudly.

"That's Marmalade," said Oscar, reappearing with his sister, who was carrying a clear plastic box filled with mud. Leah bent down to tickle Marmalade's chin.

"We've made something for you," Isabella said, thrusting the box into Leah's hands. "It's a worm farm! We've been collecting them all day."

Leah took the box hesitantly and held it at arm's length, trying not to look at the pink-skinned earthworms writhing and tunnelling in the crumbly soil.

"Thank you," she said. "I think."

Her dad checked his watch. "We'd better be off otherwise we'll miss the flight." He unloaded Leah's bags from the car and carried them to the back door.

"Be good for Freya," said her mum, kissing her cheek. "We'll see you in six weeks."

"Good luck with the lecture tour," Leah mumbled. She watched her parents' car wind its way along the twisting farm track and out of sight. A wave of homesickness washed over her. Freya patted her shoulder and smiled.

"We're so happy that you're spending the summer with us, aren't we kids?"

The twins nodded.

"We'll show you your room," said Isabella. "We've made a space for the worm farm on your bedside table. We thought you'd like them nice and close."

Leah cast one last look at the track and followed Freya and the twins into the farmhouse with heavy steps.

CHAPTER 3

Juno's Secret

Leah's room was at the back of the house, looking out onto a field of sheep. It was a small, square room with plain whitewashed walls, simple wooden furniture and red and white checked curtains. Freya had left a small vase of wild flowers on the chest of drawers. Oscar placed the worm farm on the bedside table and gazed at it lovingly.

"You need to keep the soil moist otherwise they'll dry out," he said, wiggling his fingers in the mud.

Leah shuddered. How on earth was she ever going to sleep with a boxful of worms a few centimetres from her head? Freya must have noticed her unease because she picked the box up and handed it back to her son.

"For heaven's sake Oscar, Leah doesn't want worms in her room. Keep them on the window ledge on the landing if you must." Freya fixed her son with a steely gaze and he scooted out of the room, the worm farm cradled in his arms.

Leah unzipped her suitcase. Freya waved her hand. "Leave the unpacking until later. We'll give you a guided tour of the farm and introduce you to Juno."

"Who's Juno?" Leah asked, as they crossed the farmyard past a handful of chickens enjoying a dust bath in the sunshine.

"You'll see," said Isabella, tapping her nose. "But you're going to love her."

Three goats were nibbling the grass in a small paddock to one side of the house. "Is she a goat?" Leah asked.

Isabella giggled. "No."

They passed a pig ark surrounded by a sea of mud. Snouting around in the dirt were a dozen tiny piglets who squealed with excitement when they saw Freya and the twins.

"It's not tea time yet," Oscar told them.

"Is Juno a pig?" Leah asked. Oscar shook his head and chuckled.

They walked through a field of golden wheat and another where the grass was so long it reached Leah's knees.

"We'll be cutting this for hay in the next week or so," said Freya. She pointed out the sheep and cows and showed Leah the tractor barn and the caravans where the two farmhands, Eric and Joseph, lived. Leah's new trainers were coated in grime by the time they had toured the whole farm. They were almost right back where they'd started and there was still no sign of the mysterious Juno.

Then Leah noticed a small weather-boarded building to the side of the barn. A leather headcollar was hanging on a hook beside the stable door. She crossed her fingers.

"Follow me," Isabella said, tugging Leah's hand.

They stood on tiptoes and peered into the stable. Standing in a deep bed of straw was a chestnut pony with a flaxen mane and tail. Leah clicked her tongue and the pony turned and whickered softly.

"That's Juno," said Oscar.

Juno wandered over and let Leah stroke her soft nose.

"Mum's had her since she was a foal," said Isabella proudly.

"She's beautiful," said Leah. "Horses are my favourite animals."

"I know, your mum told me," said Freya. "We all have jobs on the farm. Isabella feeds the chickens and collects the eggs. Oscar is in charge of the goats and Eric, Joseph and I look after the cattle, sheep and pigs. I thought you might like to take care of Juno while you're here."

Leah gazed at the chestnut pony. "I would love to," she breathed.

"She's got bad feet so she can't be ridden but she loves being groomed and made a fuss of, and she'll happily go for a walk on the lead rein," her godmother said.

The twins tied Juno up outside her stable and Freya eyed her critically.

"She could certainly do with the exercise. She's been on a strict diet for weeks and just keeps getting fatter and fatter. I can't understand it. If I didn't know better, I'd say you two horrors had been feeding her titbits on the sly."

Leah was surprised to see the twins shoot each other guilty looks. She turned back to Juno, whose stomach was as tight and round as a barrel. Sam had a couple of brood mares at the riding stables that produced long-legged fillies and colts every summer. Leah recognised the signs.

Juno wasn't fat. She was in foal.

Juno's Foal is available now from Amazon

ABOUT THE AUTHOR

Amanda Wills lives in Kent with her husband Adrian and sons Oliver and Thomas, and their two cats. She spent many years as a journalist and began writing children's fiction in 2013. To find out more about her books visit www.amandawills.co.uk.

30587682R00083

Printed in Great Britain
by Amazon